Jason Daly is [ ]
Jenna?

A six-inch-high mound of folders near the edge of her desk teetered, and they both lunged to stabilize the pile before it toppled to the floor. At the same time, something small and shiny fell off Jenna's desk and bounced off her sneaker.

"What was that?" Jason asked.

"Probably a paper clip."

"No," he drawled, crouching down for a closer look. "It sounded heavier, more like—ah, here it is." He rose and handed it to her. "Yours?"

She studied the diamond and ruby ring before passing to back. "No."

He examined it from several different angles. "Have you seen it before?"

She shook her head. "No, why?"

"Just wondering."

"I'll put a note on our bulletin board. Someone in our department is probably looking for it." She peered at the brilliant stones. "Pretty, isn't it?"

"Uh huh." He brought the band closer to his eyes and squinted. "There's an engraving inside."

"Really? That should help us find the owner."

Jason's furrowed brow disappeared, and his face settled into an inscrutable mask. "It definitely will. She reported it stolen."

"Stolen? Then what's it doing on *my* desk?"

He met her gaze, his eyes cool and piercing, his mouth compressed into a hard line. "That's what I'd like to know."

CATHERINE BACH is the pen name for the author of this book, set in the heartland of America. Miss Bach is familiar with the story's "Cornhusker" setting, as she lives in Kansas. Her professional education is in medical technology which adds realistic depth to her descriptions.

Thief
of My Heart

Catherine Bach

Heartsong Presents

In memory of my mother,
Hubertina Geist Werth
1929-1971

A note from the Author:
I love to hear from my readers! You may write to me at
the following address: **Catherine Bach**
Author Relations
P.O. Box 719
Uhrichsville, OH 44683

ISBN 1-57748-062-7

THIEF OF MY HEART

Cover illustration by Victoria Lisi and Julius.

PRINTED IN THE U.S.A.

prologue

"Tell me good news."

Bruce Edwards stood in front of St. Anne's business administrator and steeled himself to George Payce's demanding tone. For the first time in his career, the silver hospital security badge pinned to his uniform felt heavy, much like the responsibilities it represented. If only he did have good news to impart.

He squared his shoulders. "I'm sorry, sir."

The corners of Payce's mouth turned down and he heaved a sigh of obvious disappointment. He tossed his gold pen onto the documents spread across his massive oak desk, and leaned back in his plush, high-backed executive chair. With his bushy white eyebrows drawn into a straight line, he steepled his fingers.

"So we still have a crook roaming our halls—a crook whom we can't identify, much less put behind bars?"

"I'm afraid so," Bruce admitted, uncomfortable under Payce's green-eyed gaze. "I've increased the numbers of walk-around checks and stationed men at all the entrances, but no one has reported any suspicious characters or activity. Unless we catch him in the act, which is highly unlikely, we won't find him."

"Is he someone off the street? A disgruntled employee? A dissatisfied patient? What?"

Bruce hesitated. The only thing he knew for certain was that the man, or woman, had absconded with money and items worth thousands of dollars. Disgruntled employee? Perhaps. Greedy? Most definitely.

"The thefts occur at different times, on different shifts and in different locations," Bruce said. "Several people may be involved, not just one."

"A ring?"

"It's possible."

"Wonderful." Payce looked grim. "The Board of Directors wants this resolved soon. Our insurance company is making waves about sending in investigators, and I'm supposed to keep this *situation* out of the newspapers. We can't afford to have our clients lose faith in us and seek medical care elsewhere. Competition between the Wichita hospitals is fierce enough without this hanging over our heads."

"Yes, sir, I know. Hiring an investigator might be a good idea," Bruce offered tentatively, well-aware of Payce's penchant for cost-saving measures.

Payce's eyes narrowed. "What can he do that you can't?"

Encouraged by the lack of an outright rejection, Bruce stepped closer, intent on being his most persuasive. "Unlike myself, this person can devote every moment to solving our problem. Look at it this way. If you had cancer, you'd want an oncologist treating you, not a family practitioner. Our situation isn't any different."

Bruce added his final plea. "Even if word leaks out, having an expert involved will show everyone our commitment to finding and prosecuting the guilty party. Besides, wouldn't you rather work with an investigator of your choice?"

Staring into the distance, Payce nodded slowly, deliberately. "We have to do something. The situation can't continue for another four months." Once again, his gaze landed on Bruce. "Do you have someone in mind?"

"Jason Daly," Edwards supplied without hesitation.

A furrow appeared in Payce's forehead as he stroked his smooth-shaven chin. "The name sounds familiar."

"It should. He's the best in the business."

Payce leaned forward. "Then he's the man we want. Get him."

one

No one, until now, had ever literally taken her breath away.

Jenna Carlson croaked out the fellow's name, trying to breathe as little as possible in the presence of her newest patient. She waited a few seconds for the derelict lying on the hospital gurney to respond, but he remained silent and motionless.

"Mr. Winters," she repeated, raising her voice. She wrinkled her nose to avoid inhaling the nauseating combination of body odor, alcohol, and heaven only knew what else emanating from his person. At the same time, she wondered how many weeks it took to achieve the state of ripeness this man had so obviously reached.

She let out a long breath. What a change from the sweet-smelling newborn she'd just visited in St. Anne's nursery. After poking the infant's tiny foot for a bilirubin level, she'd cuddled the small warm bundle until sobs became little hiccups, while wishing—not for the first time—that God had seen fit to send her one of her own. Apparently her lot in life was to serve as a benevolent aunt rather than a doting mother.

Pulling her thoughts off the fruitless track they circled, she once again studied her patient. In spite of his harmless appearance, her internal alarm system screamed a warning. After working first as a phlebotomist during her college days, then as a bench medical technologist and now as a supervisor, she'd learned not to discount her inner premonitions.

"He's out of it," Shelly, the student nurse reported. "Hasn't moved a muscle in thirty minutes."

"That's comforting," Jenna replied. Based on the girl's news, she decided to proceed. She pulled the bedside table closer and laid out several blood collection tubes. With a quick twist, she cracked the seal on a sterile needle and screwed it into its holder.

O God, let him sleep, she prayed. Her experience had taught her a valuable lesson—people under the influence of alcohol and drugs usually didn't have the word "cooperation" in their vocabulary. She knew the Lord would help her, but she'd feel much better if two burly male orderlies stood nearby instead of a scrawny student nurse.

Jenna tugged on her latex gloves with a snap. "I don't believe I've seen you in E.R. before."

"Today's my first day on this rotation."

Great. She had a novice. "Well, good luck. Emergency is never dull, so you should learn a lot while you're here."

"I'm sure I will if I ever get to do something more interesting than watch this guy sleep! I wish I could have helped with the code blue we had earlier," Shelly finished wistfully.

"Well, don't worry. Your time will come."

Jenna turned back to the gurney and called the bewhiskered man by name again. "Mr. Winters, I'm going to take a blood sample now. You'll feel a little prick in your arm." Rolling up the tattered sleeve, she wrinkled her nose again.

Shelly grinned, apparently noticing Jenna's facial movements. "Overpowering, isn't he?"

Jenna nodded at the whispered comment. She'd never met anyone who needed a bath as much as this fellow did.

The girl continued in a hushed tone. "He doesn't look forty-five years old, either."

Jenna agreed. Living on the street, for whatever reason, had aged him about thirty years.

She tied the tourniquet on the man's limp arm and scrubbed the bend of his elbow with an alcohol pad. The cool disinfectant wetting his skin roused him and he began muttering and moving restlessly.

Jenna grabbed his shoulders, her words firm, yet reassuring. "Mr. Winters, just relax. No one's going to hurt you."

Winters began thrashing at his perceived attacker, spewing forty-proof curses like water from a fountain. "Get off me. Leave me alone. I want out of here!"

Shelly froze.

Jenna gripped the man's waving arms to protect herself and to prevent him from rolling off the gurney. Exasperated by the girl's hesitation, she cried, "Pull the call button, then help me. I can't hold him by myself!"

Shelly yanked on the cord, but the signal bell didn't respond with its usual irritating bleep. "It must be broken. I'll be right back." She disappeared through the curtains before Jenna could stop her.

While Jenna struggled with the furious patient alone, her supplies crashed to the floor and scattered in all directions. Ill-matched, her grip on one wriggling arm deteriorated until seconds later, he'd freed it from her determined grasp.

"I need help in here," she shouted, praying for someone, anyone, to appear.

But no one did.

Pinning one of his wiry arms to the bed with her upper body, she tried to grab the other and caught his threadbare sleeve instead. The fabric ripped.

"Just relax, Mr. Winters," she grunted. "I'm only trying to help—"

Before she could finish her sentence, he swung his unfettered arm in a pendulum motion and planted his fist against her cheekbone.

Pain burst through her head like an exploding firecracker, sending sparks in every direction. Darkness and instant nausea threatened to overtake her. In spite of her resolve, her strength ebbed and the black clouds hovering on the fringes of her vision grew larger.

ⱥ

Jason Daly verified the positioning of the emergency room's overhead closed circuit cameras against the map on his clipboard. Finding no fault with their placement, he marked several x's on the blueprint to indicate areas where added surveillance would be helpful.

An orderly brushed past him, jostling his hand. "Sorry," the man apologized as he rushed into the closest exam room carrying an IV bag.

Jason erased his inadvertent line. Perhaps he should have suggested another area of St. Anne's to begin his tour, but conditions in E.R. were unpredictable. This department's only constant was its variability.

Two nurses, in rose-colored scrub suits with stethoscopes slung around their necks, breezed by, sending a whoosh of air in his direction. Others bustled from one cubicle to the next, sending a steady stream of patients in and out. A constant hum of people's voices, cries of unhappy babies, and the creak of wheels on tiled floors filled the air. Occasionally, a telephone punctuated the background noise with a shrill and incessant demand for attention.

Once again, he studied the floor plan on his clipboard. The sooner he finished his task and Bruce Edwards returned from answering his page, the sooner they could leave this organized bedlam for quieter surroundings.

He jotted down a few notes, conscious of a thirtyish woman in the waiting room grimacing in pain, a middle-aged man in faded overalls clutching his forearm to his chest, and a doctor wearing a white coat looking harried even though it was only mid-morning.

Out of the corner of one eye, he watched another young woman, obviously a student from her uniform and hesitant actions, rush out of a curtained-off area. In the next instant, she was clutching his arm and all but pulling him in her direction.

"We need your help. A patient is going crazy. There's no one else." Her sentences were rushed and she was breathless.

In that split second, he noticed the hallways were indeed empty. He glanced toward the telephone at the nurses' station where he'd last seen Bruce. He, too, had disappeared. "Let's go."

She hurried toward their destination, Jason keeping pace with his long strides. "I don't know how long she can hold him," she said.

A crash and a loud bellow sent Jason ahead of the girl. He flung the curtains aside and saw the man on the gurney swing his arm forward. In another instant, the patient's fist made contact.

"No!" Jason shouted, hating that he'd been three steps away and a few seconds too late. He'd taken a few licks of his own during his career and didn't wish the experience on anyone, much less an unprepared woman.

"What are you doing?" he called out in his most authoritative tone. "Settle down."

By the time Jason grabbed the patient's arms and held them in a white-knuckled grip, Winters quieted. "I've got him," he told the woman whose face appeared as pale as her white lab coat. The red mark on her right cheek matched the dusky hue of her maroon scrub suit.

"Thanks," she said without moving.

In a split second, he took in her short, curly light-brown hair, simple pearl earrings, high cheekbones, and the sprinkling of freckles over her pert nose.

She shifted positions, sending a welcome whiff of a light floral fragrance in his direction. Her head came to his shoulders, making her about average height. His curiosity piqued, he studied her name tag. *Jenna Carlson, MT (ASCP), Laboratory.* His gaze fell upon her hands and an overwhelming sense of disappointment came over him.

Through the opaque latex gloves, he saw an outline of a

ring on her left hand.

Jason glanced at the student nurse standing near the foot of the bed. "You'd better find someone to move him to a more secure location." He spoke in Jenna's ear. "You can let go now. I'll take care of him."

&

I'll take care of him. Jenna couldn't remember when she'd felt so relieved.

With great care, she straightened, feeling the pain radiate through her cheek and into her right eye. Surprised by its intensity, she stumbled to the wall in search of the chair she'd seen earlier.

"Are you okay?" he asked, his concern obvious in his baritone.

She sank onto the hard seat and stripped off her gloves. It took every ounce of willpower she had to keep from slipping to the floor. Leaning against the wall, she closed her eyes and pressed a shaky hand to her head.

"Are you okay?" he repeated.

Her upset stomach gradually settled down, thanks to the cool draft coming out of the air-conditioner vent. "I think so," she answered.

A minute later, she heard the sound of running water and opened her eyes. Her rescuer—a tall, dark-haired man wearing a dark gray business suit—stood at the sink. He turned, holding a pad of wet paper towels. Without a word, he pressed his makeshift cold pack against her injured cheek. She winced.

"Sorry."

"It's okay," she said.

"I'll find Dr. Edison," Shelly offered, vanishing through the curtains once again.

"You're going to have quite a shiner."

"Why am I not surprised," Jenna replied dryly. "How's our patient?"

"Sleeping like a baby."

"Figures," she muttered.

"Still dizzy?"

She paused to evaluate her condition. "A little. Just give me a few minutes."

"Do you get this reaction every time you draw blood?" he joked.

She managed a faint smile. "If I did, I'd find another career. Seriously though, my attackers are usually five and six year olds. They don't hit quite so hard," she said ruefully.

"Be glad you're not a boxer. Maybe administration will issue combat gear for you—or at least a football helmet."

She almost laughed at the picture he painted, but the sting in her cheek ended that idea. "I'll draft a proposal right away. I'd hate for another department to get the drop on us." Imagining her boss's reaction to such a request, she grinned in spite of the ache.

"Lucky thing I was around."

"No kidding."

"I don't mean to tell you your business, but why didn't you wait for more help? People in his condition"—he motioned towards Winters— "aren't predictable."

"I know, but everyone was busy. According to Shelly, he'd been sleeping, so I thought I'd take my chances." Jenna shrugged. "I gambled and lost. Shelly moaned a few minutes ago about wanting to get involved in something exciting, but I can live without this particular kind of excitement."

"I'm sure your husband would prefer that you didn't come home looking battered and bruised."

She swallowed. The wedding ring she still wore saved her from many an unwelcome advance, which was the way she wanted it. Strangers questioning her about her husband usually received a smile and occasionally a nod of agreement. But for some reason—probably because he'd saved her from further injury—she felt constrained to tell the truth.

"I'm. . .widowed."

"I'm sorry," he murmured, his teasing smile giving way to a sympathetic demeanor. "Has it been very long?"

"Three years."

It was strange how discussing her personal life didn't seem as painful as it had in the past. Was it because of this specific man or the unusual circumstances surrounding their initial encounter? She'd give it some thought later, but at the moment, she had work to do.

Jenna staggered to her feet. The room tilted and she extended her arm to grab something solid until she regained her balance.

Grasping a handful of air, she gritted her teeth and braced herself to meet the floor. The final jolt came and she held her stiff position for a few seconds before assessing the damage. The ache in her head hadn't worsened, thank God, and lying on the tile didn't seem too bad, either.

She relaxed, waiting for the world to stop spinning. There wasn't any sense in staging a repeat performance.

A minute later, she perceived a warm, solid, textured surface under her cheek. Taking a deep breath, she tried to classify the tangy scent surrounding her. Too appealing for hospital-strength disinfectant, it reminded her of—

Men's aftershave!

She lifted her head and gazed into magnetizing hazel eyes. Shaken by his intense scrutiny, she felt as if she were a glass of water held in front of a man who'd crossed Death Valley on foot. *Oh my*, she thought, chagrined.

Seconds passed before the signals from her fingertips reached her brain, screaming the message that her arms encircled a broad chest and her hands were splayed across the man's back.

Mortified, Jenna groaned, burying her face in his shoulder. What was she doing hanging onto a strange, handsome man like a leech?

A deep voice spoke in her ear. "Are you sure you're okay? Do you want to sit down?" The strong arms surrounding her didn't relax. "Don't worry, I won't let you fall."

Uttered in a soothing tone, the words echoed in Jenna's ears. Immediately, she flashed back to her life as an eight-year-old daredevil in the Cornhusker State. She'd scaled a tree to prove to her best friend Lizzie that she could, and ended up higher than she'd planned. Her father, summoned by her frightened sidekick, had rescued Jenna by coaxing her into his arms with identical words. No one except Chad, whom she'd loved dearly since high school, had given her this sense of security.

Honestly! Pull yourself together! she scolded. Acutely aware this man wasn't a family member or her late husband, she fought the deepening blush as it spread down her face. *You're suffering from "hero" syndrome. The man saved you from being beaten to a pulp, that's all. You'd feel the same toward anyone else.*

Jenna jerked away, then held her head still, paying dearly for the sudden movement. "I'm fine," she forced out, sounding like a broken record. She bent to retrieve the scattered supplies and gasped as pain hammered at her skull.

"Let me get thôse."

She touched her forehead. "Thank you. Bending over doesn't seem to agree with me."

While he gathered the equipment strewn across the floor and under the bed, she pulled another pair of gloves out of her coat pocket and tugged them on.

Seconds later, he passed the tray to her. "It's not very neat," he apologized. "I hope I didn't overlook anything."

The strength in his fingers and the warmth of his hands set off a new shower of sparks. She swallowed hard. "It'll be fine. I'll sort through everything once I'm back in the lab."

Moving gingerly, she rose. A short time later, she retied the tourniquet on Winters' arm and prepared him for the relatively painless procedure.

"Shouldn't you wait until a doctor checks you out?" he asked.

She paused to flex her shaky hands. "Don't worry. I'm okay." After scrubbing the bend of Winters' elbow with alcohol once again, she slid the needle into the vein. This time, her inner alarm was silent, thanks to her rescuer's hovering presence.

After the last tube had filled, she heaved an audible sigh of relief and taped a cotton ball over the puncture site.

Jenna placed the used equipment on her tray, stripped off the protective latex gloves, and washed her hands with stiff, cautious motions.

Eager to escape the company of this man who, for reasons she didn't understand, now unsettled her, she grabbed her paraphernalia and addressed his chin. After almost purring in his arms like a contented kitten, she was too embarrassed to meet his gaze. "Thanks for staying. He might have started swinging again."

"No problem."

The curtain rustled, creating a welcome diversion. However, instead of the nurse Jenna had expected, Bruce Edwards' face appeared.

"I thought I heard your voice in here, Daly," Bruce said, stepping around the fabric barrier. "What are you doing— Jenna, whatever happened to you?"

She grinned at his shocked expression. "Not much. Our patient thought he was in the ring and I was a contender." Realizing the two men knew each other, she continued, "Your friend helped me out."

"We haven't had a chance to introduce ourselves," Daly inserted, his tone implying that he expected to rectify the situation immediately.

"I can fix that," Bruce declared. "Jenna, meet Jason Daly.

Jason, this is Jenna Carlson, one of our laboratory supervisors. Right now, she's also the acting department head."

Despite her intentions to hurry back to the lab and to forget this entire episode, Jenna couldn't avoid facing her benefactor without appearing rude. She hoped her first impression of a strong, handsome man had been an aberration caused by the knock on her head and he was in actuality, short and homely.

She looked directly into Jason's now-familiar hazel eyes and fought a strange desire to fidget under his probing analysis. Instead, she wrapped her composure around herself like a cloak and conducted an inspection of her own.

He had a square jaw, dark eyebrows, and thick, wavy, light brown hair which, from the tan line on his sideburns and neck, suggested it had been recently trimmed. Noting the few wrinkles around his eyes and the lack of readily discernible gray, she placed him in his late thirties.

Her gaze traveled along massive shoulders covered by a dark gray suit coat in spite of the warm June weather. His burgundy and navy tie completed the picture of a man who dressed for success.

All things considered, she had seen correctly the first time—he was anything but homely. As for being short, Jason had to be at least six inches taller than her own five and a half feet. *This guy is a real heartbreaker,* she warned herself, *and I had to literally fall all over him.*

"Pleased to meet you, Mr. Daly," she murmured, accepting the hand he'd offered. His grip was firm, yet gentle, and hard ridges lined his palm. For an instant, she wondered what physical labor was responsible for the calluses. "I appreciate everything you've done."

"My pleasure. And please call me Jason. I think we're past formality."

His boyish grin sent a flash of heat across her face. "I guess so."

As metal curtain rings scratched against the thick rod, Jenna pulled her hand free and thrust it into the side pocket of her lab coat. It wouldn't do for anyone to see how Jason's simple touch dazed her. Yet, in spite of fingering the few loose coins she carried, she couldn't dispel the tactile memory of her palm against his.

Dr. Edison, the E.R. physician, strode in. He gave the now-peaceful patient a cursory examination before conveying his orders to the two male nurses who had followed.

"Take our fellow to the Substance Abuse unit, guys," he instructed. While they wheeled a snoring Winters away, the doctor ambled toward Jenna. "So our fellow took exception to having his blood drawn. Didn't you duck fast enough?" he joked.

"Apparently not," Jenna remarked with a touch of humor. "I'm fine, though. Really."

Despite her protests, Jason confiscated the lab carryall while the doctor led her to the same stool she'd vacated moments earlier. "I have to go," she emphasized while the physician examined her face and checked her pupils. "I've already been here too long."

"Now, Jenna," Dr. Edison chided. "You know the procedure for on-the-job injuries as well as I do. The risk management people would have coronaries if I didn't take a look at you. So hush."

She let out a resigned sigh.

It wasn't long until Dr. Edison stepped back and folded his arms across his chest. "You'll end up with a black eye and a monstrous headache for a few hours, but I think you'll live." He smiled.

"I wasn't worried." Jenna gave Jason an I-told-you-so look. "Now, I need to get back to work." The sooner she left this man's unnerving presence, the sooner she'd put these strange feelings to rest. She reached for her tray, noting his solid grip on the handle.

"Do you mind if we tag along? We were headed past the lab anyway," Jason said. Although he sounded innocent, his set jaw spoke of his determination and his eyes wordlessly challenged her to make an issue in front of witnesses.

Recognizing defeat when it stared her in the face, she sighed and dropped her arm. "Sure, why not?"

His grin was victorious. He stepped back to allow her room to pass by.

Leaving the emergency room behind, she directed her next question to Bruce. "Are you showing your new employee around today?" Out of the corner of one eye, she noted how Jason fell into step on her opposite side. If she looked as bad as she felt, she couldn't fault him for thinking she'd pass out along the way.

Bruce looked sheepish. "Actually, he's my boss in a manner of speaking. It hasn't been announced officially, but George Payce hired Jason's firm to catch our crook."

"I see." Her face warmed. For some reason, knowing Jason Daly was a high-powered consultant instead of a newly-hired security guard made her memory of those minutes in his embrace even more disconcerting.

"He's the best in the business," Bruce added.

She stole a glance at the man touted as being "the best." He said nothing, but his eyes met hers and his mouth curved upward into a small smile.

Bruce's mobile pager sounded a few yards from their destination. "Can I use your phone, Jen?" he asked.

"No problem."

Once inside the lab, Jason relinquished his small burden. Jenna expected him to accompany Bruce into the secretarial office and was surprised to find him dogging her steps.

He glanced in one direction, then another. "This is quite an operation."

She scanned the huge room where the majority of testing took place and tried to see it from a newcomer's perspective. The number and variety of instruments arranged throughout the area did seem impressive, along with the large number of employees scurrying around in maroon scrub suits.

His genuine interest kept her feet rooted in one spot. She waited while he watched a robotic arm insert a needle into a lavender-capped tube, aspirate blood, then withdraw, and rinse with clear fluid.

"Amazing, isn't it?" she commented.

"I'll say."

"If you'd like, I can arrange a tour for you sometime. It usually lasts about an hour."

"I'd love it. Is tomorrow morning convenient for you?"

She blinked, then chewed on her lip. As busy as he was, she hadn't expected him to accept her offer so quickly. And she certainly hadn't intended to be his guide.

She opened her mouth to refuse, then clamped her teeth together. Considering his VIP status, surely she could spare an hour of her day.

A brunette approached. "Excuse me, Jenna, but I need your supply order."

"It's on my desk, Marian. I'll get it for you in a few minutes."

With a nod, the other woman walked away and Jenna re-addressed Jason. "I won't have any free time until late morning," she cautioned.

"No problem. How about eleven o'clock?"

"Eleven's fine. I'll see you then." She pivoted, then strode to her overburdened desk. Sighing at the sight of the uncharacteristic clutter, she began rummaging through stacks of papers. "Now if only I can find that supply order," she mumbled aloud. "I know it's here somewhere."

"Can I help?"

Her breath caught at the sound of Jason's voice and she

jumped. "I thought you'd left."

"I didn't. Can I help?" he repeated.

A refusal hovered on her lips, but the sincerity in his eyes stopped her. She shrugged. "I'm looking for a blue piece of paper." Rifling through the various notes, tablets, folders, and magazines on her desk, she made a mental note to order a few organizer trays.

"Is this it?" He tugged on a sheet half-hidden by a telephone message and a current issue of a laboratory management journal.

"Perfect!" she cried, feeling the tension leave her shoulders. "It took two hours to compile the information and I'd hate to redo it."

A six-inch-high mound of folders near the edge of her desk teetered, and they both lunged to stabilize the pile before it toppled to the floor. At the same time, something small and shiny fell off Jenna's desk and bounced off her sneaker.

"What was that?" Jason asked.

"Probably a paper clip."

"No," he drawled, crouching down for a closer look. "It sounded heavier, more like—ah, here it is." He rose and handed it to her. "Yours?"

She studied the diamond and ruby ring before passing it back. "No."

He examined it from several different angles. "Have you seen it before?"

She shook her head. "No, why?"

"Just wondering."

"I'll put a note on our bulletin board. Someone in our department is probably looking for it." She peered at the brilliant stones. "Pretty, isn't it?"

"Uh huh." He brought the band closer to his eyes and squinted. "There's an engraving inside."

"Really? That should help us find the owner."

Jason's furrowed brow disappeared, and his face settled into an inscrutable mask. "It definitely will. She reported it stolen."

"Stolen? Then what's it doing on *my* desk?"

He met her gaze, his eyes cool and piercing, his mouth compressed into a hard line. "That's what I'd like to know."

A horrifying thought flashed into Jenna's mind and fear settled in the pit of her stomach like a huge boulder. *No*, she screamed inwardly, feeling her heart rate speed up from the adrenaline "fight-or-flight" surge. One hand flew to her throat. Surely he didn't think. . .

But she read it in his eyes.

Jason thought she was the thief.

two

Jenna straightened her spine. "*I* certainly didn't take it."

"You'd better come with me," Jason said.

With a sinking heart, she realized that the Jason Daly with a remarkable sense of humor had disappeared. In his place stood a grim, hard-nosed, don't-play-tricks-with-me investigator— one who wouldn't have any qualms about slapping her in handcuffs if she refused to cooperate.

To add further insult to injury, her face throbbed in time to her rapid heartbeat, and she had a headache strong enough to flatten Superman. Her day had slowly but surely turned from bad to worse and it wasn't even lunch time.

O Lord, help me!

"Can I at least give this list to Marian and grab some aceta-minophen first?" she asked, sounding calmer and more con-trolled than the knots in her stomach indicated.

He nodded, his hazel eyes as cold as a Kansas winter.

At least he isn't heartless, she thought. "Where are we going, by the way?"

"My office."

A measure of relief swept over her—she didn't want to think about a drive to the police station. For the next few minutes, she attended to only the most pressing matters, making a trip to the lounge her last priority. There, she swallowed a few pain relievers and retrieved an ice pack, conscious of Jason's shad-owing presence.

Does he think I'll make a run for it? she silently grumbled, her original fear now tempered with indignation. *Aren't peo-ple innocent until proven guilty?*

With his guiding hand under her elbow, he walked beside her until they reached the secretaries' office where Bruce had parted company a short time before.

Bruce will straighten this all out, she chanted in her mind, trying to hide her worry. She must have been unsuccessful because the moment she met him in the hallway, his cheerful expression faded.

"Do you have a few minutes?" Jason asked.

Bruce looked puzzled. "Sure. What's up?"

"A new development," Jason answered, his tone noncommittal. "I'll fill you in when we get to the office."

The walk took place in silence and was blessedly brief. Jenna sank onto a wooden chair opposite Jason's desk and held her spine stiff. While Jason updated Bruce on his find, she pressed the ice bag to her face and blocked everything out of her mind except the pain. Once the men turned their attention to her, she dropped the cold pack on her lap.

"I didn't steal the ring," she reiterated, directing her affirmation toward Bruce and ignoring Jason.

Out of the corner of her eye, she saw Jason move from the filing cabinet to sit behind his desk. He skimmed through pages in a folder—obviously his reports about the stolen goods.

"Now, Jenna, no one's accusing you," Bruce soothed. "We need to learn how and why it ended up on your desk."

"I can't help you. I've never seen it before in my life," she repeated.

"Where were you yesterday morning at seven-fifteen?" Jason asked.

"I'm not sure. Any number of places, I suppose," she snapped, perturbed that Jason didn't seem to accept her innocence like Bruce did.

Her sharp tone didn't seem to make an impression. "What time did you come to work?" Jason asked.

"Six A.M."

"And?"

"And, I grabbed a pile of specimen labels for the third and fourth floor patients. By the time I finished my rounds it was seven-thirty, give or take a few minutes."

"Were you the only one from your department on the fourth floor?" Bruce asked.

"Probably. We divide the collection requests between the early morning phlebotomists. Since we were short a person, I covered both units."

"This ring was taken from a woman on four west. Room 459 to be exact," Jason stated.

"I don't remember going there. Besides, all of my patients in that unit were men," she finished on a triumphant note. Anticipating his next question, she added, "I happen to remember because it was so unusual."

"Where were you before you found the ring?" he fired back, obviously undaunted by the disclosure of her minor, but in her eyes, significant detail.

"I went to ICU this morning and after I returned, I stayed in the lab. I compiled the list of supplies for Marian. The blue list," she reminded him.

Jason frowned. "So you have no idea when it might have landed on your desk."

"Exactly. With handling the extra paperwork while my boss is on vacation, you're lucky I found it today and not sometime during the next century."

"It didn't walk from room 459 to your desk by itself," Jason said. "Someone put it there—probably someone whose presence wouldn't be considered unusual at either location. That fact eliminates a fair number of people, but it moves the folks in your department to the top of the suspect list."

She returned his gaze. "Namely me?"

"If you were in my position, what would you think?" he countered.

"Well, you're wrong. I'm not involved and I'd vouch for my employees. I don't care how the situation looks. Appearances can be deceiving."

"My point exactly," he drawled.

His implication cut her to the quick. Twirling her wedding band, she lowered her gaze and blinked rapidly to relieve the burning sensation behind her eyes.

Bruce leaned one hip against a small table. "Do you know of anyone who's having financial difficulties? Anyone living beyond their means?"

Suddenly weary, she positioned the ice pack on her aching face. "No."

"Jason is right," Bruce said. "Anyone can have a good reason for being in a patient's room, but your department doesn't see a lot of extraneous hospital traffic. Non-laboratory people stand out like sore thumbs."

Jenna conceded the point.

"Have you noticed anyone hanging around who shouldn't be there?" Bruce asked.

She closed her eyes to think. "I haven't, but maybe someone else has. I'll ask around."

Bruce rose, signaling for Jenna to do likewise. "I think we can let you get back to work. Call us if you remember anything else."

"I will." Jenna turned on her heel and left the room, anxious to escape. Although Bruce had believed her story, Jason hadn't been convinced of her innocence. She was still his prime suspect.

❧

Jason slung his suit coat over the swivel chair's back and folded his arms across his white-shirted chest. "She's our best lead so far."

Bruce grimaced. "You'll never convince me she's responsible."

"Really?" Jason pictured Jenna's short, curly, maple syrup-colored hair, pert nose, and heart-shaped face with little effort. What stood out in his mind, however, were the sparks of indignation shooting out of her dark brown eyes after he'd voiced his suspicions concerning her colleagues. A woman with strong loyalties and intense feeling obviously hid underneath her cool, professional attitude.

He took a deep breath, savoring the faint traces of her scent. The fragrance was etched in his memory, especially since he'd liberally inhaled it while he'd held her in the emergency room—the same scent that had enabled him to endure the derelict's pungent aroma.

Recalling each moment in vivid detail, he also remembered the softness of her skin, the way she nestled in his embrace, the feel of her hair against his chin. He wouldn't mind repeating that particular experience over and over again.

"How well do you know her?"

"She's a good friend." Bruce's voice lacked any note of possessiveness.

Encouraged, Jason pressed on. "She mentioned her husband died, but what else can you tell me?"

Bruce's eyes widened. "*She* told you that?"

"Yeah."

"When?"

"In E.R. While we were waiting for the doctor. Why are you surprised? Is it a secret or something?"

"No, but Jenna normally lets men think she's married. Claims she doesn't want to get involved again."

How interesting. Jason raised one eyebrow in a wordless query for more information.

Bruce obliged. "Her husband was a highway patrol officer. He'd pulled a car over for speeding and the driver shot him."

"Bummer." The information revived a memory of being the bearer of similar bad news to the wives of men he'd worked with on the police force. The children's expressions had hurt the worst.

Jason swallowed the bitter lump in his throat. "Any kids?"

Bruce shook his head. "No. Work became her outlet, along with her faith. She doesn't socialize much, although she does participate in group activities—like St. Anne's softball team."

While part of Jason wanted to accept Bruce's assessment of Jenna's upstanding character and his instincts encouraged him to do so, his training reminded him to concentrate on the evidence at hand.

"Could she be unhappy with her job, or the hospital as a whole?"

Bruce shook his tawny head. "First of all, she isn't a vengeful person. Second, she hasn't been at St. Anne's very long— about six months."

"Isn't that when your troubles began?"

"Yes, but Jenna is definitely not behind this. You can't convince me otherwise."

Hearing the insistence in his partner's voice, Jason decided to tread lightly. "Regardless, it's an interesting coincidence, and I can't ignore one crucial fact—I found stolen goods in her possession."

"Jenna's a fine, Christian woman. I know people who call themselves by that name, yet they don't observe the law. Jenna, however, is committed to her faith. She's made it clear that if she ever considers a relationship again, it will be with someone who shares her beliefs."

The news made Jason smile. What were the odds of two complete strangers wanting a similar fellowship and meeting in a town this size outside of a church-sponsored activity?

Something about Jenna Carlson had touched a chord in him from the moment he'd held her. Firmly convinced of God's ability to rule events and be in control, he knew he hadn't met Jenna by accident. It remained to be seen, however, if she was the answer to his personal prayer for a life partner, or the party he was supposed to bring to justice.

One thing was certain—he needed to check out her story. She was the only suspect he had.

ɞ

Jenna frowned, studying the packing slips and invoices arrayed across her desk. After twenty-four hours, her headache had disappeared although an occasional twinge reminded her of the incident. As predicted, the purplish bruise under her eye had developed into a colorful shade of violet, although makeup had softened its brightness.

She rested her chin on one palm and rubbed her gold wedding band with her thumb. Even now, a day later, it still irked her how readily Jason Daly suspected her of stealing the ring. True, the ring's appearance on her desk didn't corroborate her innocence, but after hearing her story, he should have believed her. He was a hot-shot investigator—couldn't he tell when a person told the truth?

Engrossed in her mental reenactment of their confrontation, she hardly noticed Sam, one of her supervisees, nonchalantly saunter by.

"Brass at three o'clock," he whispered, journeying toward the flammable materials cabinet in a roundabout manner.

Jenna turned her head in the direction he'd indicated. The sight of Jason surveying the lab made her heart pound. Whatever was he doing here? Hadn't he grilled her enough yesterday? An instant urge to slip away spread over her, but she knew her efforts were futile. He'd catch up to her eventually.

Grateful for Sam's warning, she tidied a few papers on her desk and tried to quiet the butterflies fluttering in her stomach.

She took a deep breath, and chided herself for her nervousness. After all, she was an efficient professional who also happened to be innocent of any wrongdoing. And she definitely wouldn't let herself remember how wonderful his embrace had felt.

She scooted her chair away from the desk. In spite of her resolve to present an unconcerned demeanor, her knees shook as she rose to greet him.

"Good morning, Jenna," Jason remarked, his pearly white teeth glimmering in his smile.

"What can I do for you?" she answered, wincing at her uncharacteristic frosty tone.

He tapped his watch crystal. "It's eleven. We had an appointment. Remember?"

Her mind drew a blank for only a second. "Oh, yes. It slipped my mind. Too busy, I guess."

"If this isn't a good time. . ." he began.

"No, it's okay." Canceling the tour was an attractive option, but she would only prolong the inevitable. As tenacious as he seemed to be, he'd return again and again until he got what he wanted.

"How's your head today?"

"Fine," she answered, wary of his friendly overture. "Over-the-counter pain relievers work wonders." She lowered her voice as she led him toward the chemistry processing station. "No one has reported seeing any unauthorized people in their areas."

"Thanks for checking. What's this machine for?"

Taking his cue to avoid discussing the case—at least not here and now—she began to explain the purpose of the refrigerated floor centrifuge. Talking to the public about the lab's role in medicine had long been one of her favorite tasks, so as the tour progressed, her initial animosity gave way to a more congenial attitude.

While she led Jason around the department, she couldn't help but notice the number of female heads turning in his direction. Although visitors such as repairmen and salesmen were commonplace, she couldn't recall any other stranger generating such a high degree of curiosity among the staff.

She also kept a close eye on Jason's body language during her presentation. His attentive expression and intelligent questions suggested a genuine interest in the inner workings of a clinical laboratory. Then again, he might be working undercover, looking for more evidence to use against her. She frowned at the unwelcome thought.

"Something wrong?" he asked.

Jenna blinked, startled out of her worries by his question. "No. I, um, just thought of something. It isn't important," she finished lamely.

She ushered him to the last stop—a room directly off the main lab. "This is our blood bank. Our units come from the regional American Red Cross which, fortunately for us, is local. We stock all the blood types, but we keep more of the common ones, like O and A positive. Now you've seen the entire department. Any questions?" she asked.

"No," he replied, "but I have something to confess."

Confess? Her stomach churned. Had he feigned curiosity in order to gather more evidence against her? She buried her hands in her lab coat pockets, balling them into tight fists until her fingernails bit into her palms.

With sheer force of will, she presented a composure totally at odds with her inner turmoil. She raised one eyebrow. "Really?"

The sight of his apologetic face didn't diminish her fears. He continued. "I had an ulterior motive for coming today, but don't get me wrong, I also wanted to learn about the lab."

Her face froze. With her heart pounding out a drum roll, her breath caught in her throat. "Oh?"

"Yeah." He shifted positions. "We'd shared a unique experience in Emergency and I'd hoped our camaraderie would continue. Unfortunately, I think we lost it when I found the ring on your desk. Wouldn't you agree?"

Without smiling, she nodded once, then crossed her arms. "Getting the third degree wasn't exactly an endearing event, nor one I'd care to repeat."

"I know. Can you chalk yesterday afternoon up to me simply doing my job? I'd like for us to start over."

Jenna blinked, hardly believing what she'd heard. After envisioning the worst, she'd never expected him to say what he had. "What?"

"Can we start over? Pretend we're meeting today for the first time?"

His candor surprised her. She let out the breath she'd been holding. Yet, there was one wrinkled detail she needed to iron out.

"Am I still a suspect?"

"I don't think you stole Mrs. Harris' ring," Jason recited, holding up one hand. "If you'd like, I have a Bible in my car. I could—"

She smiled. "That won't be necessary."

He extended his hand. "Friends?"

She stared at his open palm, then slowly, she met his steady gaze. He might have offered the proverbial olive branch to mask a hidden agenda, but his eyes seemed to shine with honesty and sincerity. Suddenly, she knew what she had to do. If he could humble himself, she could forgive.

"Friends," she said, placing her hand in his. The simple gesture, the touch of his rough fingers against hers, the face-splitting grin on his tanned face, sent a surge of joy into her heart. It reaffirmed her decision to not hold a grudge.

"You won't regret it," he promised.

As he smiled down at her with a lopsided grin, she almost wished he had asked for something more personal than a casual friendship. Yet, it was for the best that he hadn't. His profession, although not as dangerous as other law enforcement careers, still dealt with the criminal element. She refused to tie herself emotionally to a man who faced death on a daily basis.

She wouldn't risk burying another husband in the prime of his life.

❧

With his spirits high, Jason strode toward his temporary office in St. Anne's Security Department. Although Jenna didn't seem the type to renege on an appointment—even after the unpleasant circumstances of yesterday—the tiniest doubt had taunted him. Now he was glad: glad that he'd been able to establish a more solid footing with her, and glad that his character assessment had been correct.

He also had another reason for his good mood. His encounter with Jenna had been refreshing. Like a 150-watt bulb illuminating a dark room at the flick of a switch, his outlook on life had flipped nearly a hundred-and-eighty degrees.

After Suzanne, he'd been like a dormant tree in winter. His feelings had gone underground, as if waiting for the right conditions to come back to life. Now, with a small and slightly rickety footbridge built over the chasm separating them, his heart raced with anticipation and an excitement he hadn't experienced in a long time.

He'd wanted to press onward, ask her to dinner, to a movie, to *something,* but the atmosphere and timing hadn't been quite right. Battering down her resistance required a more relaxed setting than her workplace.

As much as he wanted to get to know her on a more personal level, he also had his investigation to consider. He'd told the truth earlier—he *didn't* believe she'd stolen the ring, but its appearance on her desk was too coincidental to suit him.

Cultivating a relationship with Jenna seemed his best course of action. He had two good reasons for doing so, although he wouldn't admit which one was more important. Nevertheless, he was both excited and impatient to put his plan into motion.

❧

Jenna preferred a late lunch break because by one o'clock, the cafeteria traffic had usually slowed to a trickle. Today, however, was an exception.

Scouting for an empty place, she spied one on the right side of the room. A few steps from her destination, she recognized the person seated across from the vacant chair.

A wave of uncertainty washed over her and she stopped short. In the next instant, Jason glanced in her direction. A slow smile spread across his features and he beckoned her with a wave. Hesitantly, she walked forward.

He rose, holding his paper napkin with one hand and motioning with the other. "Have a seat."

"Thanks."

"Long time no see," he deadpanned.

"Yeah, right. What's it been? A whole hour?" she replied, following his teasing lead.

"Give or take fifteen minutes. Has business slowed down for you?"

"Afraid not." Unnerved by his close presence, she ripped into her package of sour cream and onion-flavored potato chips with more force than necessary. An entire seam burst, spraying chips everywhere. To her consternation, a few also sailed into Jason's ham and bean special.

Inwardly she cringed and wanted to melt into the floor. "Sorry about that."

Jason took a bite. "You may have invented a new dish. This isn't too bad."

He handled that faux pas well, she thought. "What about you? Any new developments, Mr. Daly?"

His brow arched. "Back to formality?"

Her face warmed. As much as she wanted—no, *needed*—to keep some distance, friends didn't call each other by their titles. "Sorry. Forgive me?" As an afterthought, she added, "Jason."

His now-familiar lopsided grin reappeared. "How could I possibly refuse?"

With a flash of insight, Jenna understood how Jason Daly had become so successful. Hiding his persistence under an easygoing manner allowed him to obtain more information than if he came across gruff and unbending.

"To answer your question," he continued, "there aren't any recent developments. We'll change a few things in the hospital's security system and procedures. It's only a matter of time until the case is solved."

"I'm sure Payce will be pleased to hear that." She sipped her lemonade, hoping the culprit was some stranger and not one of her colleagues moonlighting as a thief.

"Any plans this evening?"

She nodded. "A softball game. Women's slow-pitch."

"Really? What position do you play?"

"Left field."

"Then I don't suppose I could interest you in dinner?"

Stalling for time, she took another sip. She'd been half-afraid he'd ask and half-afraid he wouldn't. In any case, she gave the only answer she could. "Sorry. We play at six."

"How about afterwards?"

"I don't think so."

"Tomorrow night, then?"

"Jason," she began gently. "I'm flattered that you asked, but I can't go out with you."

"I see." He paused. "Is there someone else?"

She bit the inside of her mouth. "No. I just don't date people I work with."

"We're not working together," he said, clearly surprised by her comment. "Testing blood samples isn't my thing."

"I don't get involved with people from the hospital, okay?" Her curt answer bordered on rudeness, but she had to make her point. Besides, she didn't have to justify her personal life or her decisions to anyone except God.

"I'm not a hospital employee."

"You're on contract as a consultant. Same difference."

"Temporary consultant," he corrected. "I only asked about supper. We don't have to call it a date."

His invitation was appealing. Her resolve weakened. Yet. . . "I'm sorry, but I can't."

A pleasant-sounding female voice came over the PA system. "Jenna Carlson, Jenna Carlson. Please call 4230."

Thankful for the reprieve, she rose. "So much for lunch. See you around." Without giving him a chance to say a word, she hurried toward the phone. A minute later, she deposited her tray on the conveyor belt and gave thanks for her timely reprieve.

He'd never know how close her resistance had come to crumbling.

&

The late afternoon meeting with George Payce went as well as Jason had expected; the administrator was anxious for the hospital's troubles to be resolved and he vocalized the sentiment often. After reassuring the man countless times, Jason was ready for the workday to officially end.

"Are you doing anything this evening?" Bruce asked as they walked out of the hospital.

Jason slung his coat over one shoulder and stripped off his tie. "Nothing worth mentioning."

"Want to go to a softball game?" Bruce asked.

Jason's interest perked. "St. Anne's?"

Bruce nodded. "If our team wins I promised my sister, Abby, a celebration supper. You're welcome to join us."

"Sounds great."

After a quick trip home to exchange his suit for tan walking shorts and a short-sleeved navy polo shirt, Jason drove to Bruce's home. On Bruce's suggestion, he'd agreed to carpool to the sports complex.

The two men entered the stands just as the scoreboard changed to the fifth inning. The air reverberated with cheers, yells, and catcalls while the wooden bleachers thundered under stomping feet. The early evening breeze carried the smell of popcorn and hot dogs, enticing hungry fans to visit the concession stand.

"Look at that score! These games are always exciting, but when the two hospitals are pitted against each other, everyone's out for blood." Bruce leaned toward Jason in order to be heard. "I wish Payce hadn't been so long-winded. The first innings must have been something to see."

Bruce spied two vacant seats while Jason watched St. Anne's team, wearing white jerseys and royal blue shorts, hustle onto the field. The first batter cracked a fly ball into left field. Number twelve caught it with ease and threw it to the shortstop. Having played on a men's team and being a baseball fan himself, Jason recognized talent when he saw it.

"Jen is good out there, isn't she?" Bruce yelled over the crowd's roar.

Jason nodded, then followed Bruce up the bleachers.

The next batter connected with the ball, sending it sailing toward the left field line. Jenna raced to the foul line, her attention riveted on the descending softball.

Crossing the baseline, she reached out her gloved hand.

"She's too close to the fence," Jason called out, craning his neck for a better view.

In the next instant, she crashed into the chain-link barrier. Remembering his own experiences with unyielding fences, he winced.

To his dismay, Jenna somersaulted twice on the grass before coming to a full stop.

A moment passed. Then another.

He waited for her to rise, but she remained on the ground, lying deathly still.

three

Jason jumped up. Hardly breathing, he imagined a multitude of injuries—all of them serious.

Others apparently came to the same conclusion. The frenzy died down as quickly as it had erupted and a hush spread through the park.

St. Anne's center fielder ran toward Jenna and knelt at her side. From the quick way the girl ran her hands over Jen's body, Jason guessed she'd suffered no broken bones. Jenna was rolled onto her side before the other players gathered around their fallen comrade.

More minutes ticked by. Impatient for a medical verdict, he remained standing, his body tense. At long last, two women helped Jenna to her feet. He didn't sit again until she walked to the dugout under her own power, accompanied by the coach and several players.

"That was quite a catch," Jason remarked over the crowd's cheers, hearing his own relief. He didn't realize until that moment how tense he'd become worrying if Jenna had been hurt. None of the other women he dated would have played so aggressively, if at all. *I wonder if she's really all right?*

Only a few days ago, a man nearly knocked her out. Today, a lousy ball game threatened to do the same. What would tomorrow bring? He gritted his teeth.

Meanwhile, his attention on the dugout activity never wavered. From the way she hit the fence, she had to have suffered more than a few scrapes.

"Shouldn't she see a doctor?" he asked, watching another player bandage her arm.

"Nearly every department in the hospital is represented down there," Bruce remarked. "Someone should be able to tell if she needs more than first aid."

Observing Jen's grimaces, Jason decided to remove her from the field himself if further untoward events occurred.

Bruce cleared his throat. "Worried?"

The comment shocked Jason like a bucket of ice water dumped on his head. No ties bound them together. So why was he concerned over her health? He managed a tight grin. "Guess so."

"She'll be fine. She's tough."

True, he thought, recalling the days since he'd met her. Not many people would have held up under the strain of being attacked and then interrogated as a possible suspect. She was obviously a person used to relying on herself. If she hadn't possessed the trait prior to her husband's tragedy, she'd certainly acquired it afterwards.

He thought back to lunch. Jenna had been on the brink of accepting his dinner invitation; he'd seen it in her eyes. For a few seconds, he'd caught a glimpse of fear underneath her confident demeanor. Was she afraid of Jason Daly the investigator, or Jason Daly, the man?

Her hasty departure had granted her a reprieve. Little did she know it would only be a short one.

❧

Jenna leaned her head against the backrest and prayed for the game to end. Since they were short of substitutes, she dreaded the possibility of overtime innings. Her arm and elbow throbbed at the idea of batting again.

Thirty-two is definitely too old for this kind of abuse, she thought. Idly, she glanced toward the crowd and to her surprise, saw Bruce and Jason seated beside each other. She tensed, momentarily forgetting the ache in her arm. Why was Jason turning up everywhere she went?

The opposing team made quick work of their offense and one, two, three, St. Anne's team rushed to the outfield. Jenna resigned herself to the inevitable and flexed her sore arm as she walked to her position.

Luckily, the next three hits never left the infield and Jenna returned to the dugout ready for her turn at bat.

A ball sailing to right field got her to first base and the next two batters advanced her to third. With two outs, she had to score. The pitcher wound up and she prepared for a mad dash if the opportunity arose.

Another hit to right field sent her scurrying toward home. She dove into the batter's box, both hands reaching for the plate. Sliding to a stop, she stared up at the umpire through the cloud of dust. His waving arms revealed his decision.

Safe.

The crowd roared. Jenna's cohorts hoisted her to her feet and clapped her on the back.

Ecstatic fans poured onto the field. After consoling the losers, Jenna limped her way to the dugout.

"Good game, Jenna," Lydia Austin, a passing acquaintance from the opposing hospital, said.

"It was exciting, wasn't it?"

"Yeah. But we'll win next time," Lydia promised with a smile. She disappeared in the crowd a few seconds before Jason appeared at Jenna's side.

"Good job," he praised.

"Thanks. We have a great team, don't we?" She lifted a half-empty bottle of a grape-flavored sports drink to her mouth and drained its contents.

"Who taught you to slide?" he asked.

She tossed the plastic bottle into her duffel bag. "My brothers. Rick and Trenton are diehard players. They're also volunteer coaches for the youth baseball program back home in Grand Island." She dropped her mitt inside the bag, next to her pocket pager, practice balls, and first aid kit.

"I saw you limping. Are you all right?" The furrow in his brown suddenly cleared and his lopsided smile returned. "That's all I ever ask you, isn't it?"

She grinned. "Now that you mention it. . ."

Abby Edwards, Jenna's best friend, appeared with Bruce in tow. "Are you ready for that steak Bruce promised us?"

Jenna hesitated. She was tired, sweaty, and her whole body ached. "I'll pass this time."

Abby planted her hands on her hips. "Now, Jen, you said this morning that you didn't have anything planned tonight. This victory is a feather in our cap, and we need to celebrate."

"You don't have to stay late," Bruce added.

Jason uttered one word. "Please."

The quiet caress in his voice sent warm shivers down her spine.

"Okay, okay, you've convinced me, if for no other reason than to stop your begging. But first I'm going home to shower, and you can't blame me if I fall asleep while I'm eating. See you in about an hour."

Jenna strolled away. By the time she'd covered a few yards, Jason had materialized beside her.

"May I drive you home? I'm a very good chauffeur. Took first in my defensive driving class."

"Expecting a high-speed chase on the way out of the parking lot?" she asked, her tone dry.

He laughed. "No. Just a lot of fans who are in a hurry to go home. Besides, it will give you an opportunity to unwind."

Staring into his face, Jenna fought a sudden impulse to smooth his wind-blown hair. Instead, she clutched the handle of her duffel bag. "What about your car?"

"I caught a ride with Bruce, so I'm totally at your mercy." Jason's pleading tone contradicted the sparkle in his eyes.

Realizing that her two friends were nowhere in sight,

understanding dawned. "Abby's afraid I'll call and cancel, so she sent you to make sure I wouldn't. Am I right?"

"Guilty as charged. How did you know?"

His amazement made her grin. "Experience and intuition. Abby hates it when I spend an evening alone, although this is the first time she's planned my travel arrangements."

"So, do I go with you or do I have to walk?" His face took on a sad, puppy-in-the-window look.

"Well. . . ," she drawled, making a point to stare at his name-brand running shoes. She pretended to deliberate the matter but her smile ruined the long-suffering effect she tried to achieve.

She dug in her pocket for her keys. "Here, catch," she said, impressed as he snatched the key ring in mid-air with one hand. Waving in the general direction, she continued, "My car's over there somewhere. I'll warn you, though. I haven't been home much the past few weeks, so if you're expecting Suzy Home-maker, you're in for a surprise."

He snapped his fingers. "Lucky for you, I left my white gloves in my other pair of shorts."

They located her car and she waited while he unlocked the door. After she was settled in the passenger's seat, he walked to the driver's side and slid behind the wheel. Pitying his cramped legs, Jenna leaned over to point out the seat adjustment.

"The lever has a tendency to stick," she said. "Next time I take my car in for service, I'll have the guys see if they can fix the problem."

He reached down and his hand brushed hers as he located the mechanism. As before, pleasant tingles shot up her arm and a disturbing thought crossed her mind. How would she keep this evening on a platonic, unemotional level?

She pulled her hand free and clutched her hands in her lap. Hiding her discomfort, she recited her address as they joined the line of cars exiting the grounds.

With her next breath, she blurted out, "I've been thinking

about the ring appearing on my desk, Jason. I hope you haven't focused your investigation on my staff. Nursing personnel, physicians, a few respiratory therapy, and pharmacy people come to the lab all the time, not to mention the maintenance and housekeeping people. Why, even the pink ladies and candy stripers wander through."

"I see your point, but we're only in the inquiry phase. We haven't limited ourselves to any one area."

Comforted by his reply, she relaxed. "You really think you'll catch the guy before he moves on to greener pastures?"

"I'm positive."

She analyzed the inflection he placed on his sentence. He had stated a fact without any undertones of arrogance, confident in his own and his staff's abilities.

"What made you become a security consultant?"

He turned the corner onto her street in a perfectly executed maneuver. "It's rather involved, but when I was a kid, someone quoted a statistic that indicated most people usually retired at whatever job they held when they were thirty. It doesn't apply now like it did then, but when I hit the big three-oh, I re-evaluated my likes, dislikes, and priorities.

"I'd worked burglary for a long time and saw a need for a security business—one to tailor security measures to each client, whether they were businessmen or homeowners. Crime prevention was always a focus of mine, so it seemed logical to focus my pursuits in that direction. Since then, I've hired other people with similar backgrounds in police work, so we also perform private investigations for individuals and companies."

"Like St. Anne's?"

"Like St. Anne's," he reaffirmed. "Generally, we take on an advisory role, but once in a while and depending on the situation, top management will give us carte blanche. That's what is so exciting—the variety."

"You had an excellent idea."

"I thought so, but at the time, my fiancée didn't. Suzanne called off our engagement after I turned in my resignation. She had higher ambitions of my rising someday to the illustrious position of police chief." He continued matter-of-factly. "At the same time, we couldn't reconcile our religious beliefs or our ideas about a family. I was glad those things came to light before we tied the knot."

"You were fortunate," she agreed. "At the beginning of our marriage, Chad didn't agree that a personal relationship with Jesus was necessary. As a result, we endured some rocky times. Providentially, he had a change of heart and accepted Christ about a year before he died."

Jason parked in front of her small home located in the middle of a circle drive. "This looks like a well-kept neighborhood."

"It is. I love the shade trees in every yard, especially my lilac bushes. The only thing I'd change is to add a garage. I hate to scrape ice."

She scampered out of the car, refusing to wait for him to open her door. This could hardly be called a date and she didn't want to treat it as one, yet his impeccable manners were more suited for a romantic evening. He insisted on carrying her duffel bag and unlocked the front door for her.

"Make yourself at home," she said before disappearing into her bedroom. "There's iced tea and pop in the fridge. Cookies are in the cookie jar."

Jason helped himself to a can of lemonade and a cookie. Spying a potpourri pot on the kitchen counter, he realized the strawberry scent pervading the air originated here.

With that mystery solved, he ambled back into the spacious living room containing a sofa, a recliner, and an entertainment center. Her decorating tastes leaned toward the Early American style just as his did—a far cry from Suzanne's preferences for glass and chrome.

He scanned her CD selection, noticing her selection of

Christian music outnumbered secular music almost three to one. She had a wide variety of books, ranging from Christian guidance to a best-selling romance novel. A well-worn Bible rested on her coffee table.

A basket of peach, beige, and blue yarn, knitting needles, and what appeared to be the beginnings of an afghan stood in the corner behind the recliner. No doubt she'd made the white lap robe covering the back of the sofa.

Overall, the room projected a quiet, unassuming atmosphere, similar to the woman who'd created it. Although he'd only seen her in shapeless scrub suits, lab coats, and now a baseball uniform, he doubted she owned anything ostentatious.

Before he could make any other discoveries, Jenna appeared in the doorway. "Hope I didn't take too long," she said, sounding breathless.

"Not at all," he remarked, noting her long denim skirt, red shirt, and the simple gold chain around her neck. Inordinately pleased by his accuracy, he drained his drink with a long swallow to keep a satisfied grin off his face.

He couldn't believe his luck. Jenna Carlson seemed to be the woman he'd been praying for.

❧

Jenna laid the knife and fork across her plate and leaned back in the patio chair. "That was absolutely delicious."

"I agree," Jason added. "I'll be happy to accept another invitation."

"I must admit my brother knows his way around a grill," Abby said, clearing away the dishes. "Of course he still doesn't know how to work the dishwasher, washing machine, vacuum—"

"It's dangerous to harass the cook," Bruce reminded her cheerfully. "Don't you know that?"

Abby rolled her eyes and pretended horror.

"Have you two always lived here?" Jason asked, amused by their antics.

"Oh no," Abby told him, becoming serious. "Our grandmother left us this house in her will. Since we both found jobs here in Wichita, we decided not to sell. It's been a great way to save on expenses. Plus, we don't have the hassles of roommates."

"If one of us marries, the other will buy out his or her half," Bruce finished.

"Speaking of marriage, Bruce," Jenna teased, "I saw Lydia at the game. Have you asked her out yet?"

Bruce's fair complexion turned ruddy. "Yes."

"That's wonderful," she exclaimed.

"Lydia works at St. Mark's Hospital on the three-to-eleven shift," Bruce mentioned for Jason's benefit, "and we don't go out as often as I'd like. It's hard to get our free time to coincide. She's a med tech like Abby and Jenna."

"Well, if she's the right one, don't give up," Jenna advised, loading a tray with dirty dishes. "God can work around schedules, just like that." She snapped her fingers before picking up the tray.

Jason bounded to his feet and slid open the door for the two women. "Need any help?"

"Everything's under control," Jenna said.

"We'll be right back with dessert," Abby added as she followed her inside, carrying an empty iced tea pitcher and several dirty serving bowls. She plunked the dishes into the sink and turned to Jenna.

"I haven't seen you this relaxed in a long time," she commented.

Jenna smiled as she sliced the ice cream cake Jason had contributed to the meal. On their way over, he'd stopped at the closest ice cream shop and confessed to his weakness for ice cream.

"Don't get a swelled head, Abby, but I'm glad I came."

"Have you noticed how Jason directs his attention to you? He's really interested."

A wave of shyness descended upon Jenna. "I noticed, but I'm not ready for an intense relationship."

"Do me a favor. *Get ready.* And if he asks you out, say yes."

Before Jenna could utter a word, a smug-looking Abby thrust the dessert tray in her hands and ushered her outside.

An hour later, Jenna's beeper sounded. "Sorry," she told the group assembled on the patio, "but I have to call it a night."

"What do they want, now?" Abby fussed. "How many hours did you work last week?"

"For your information, mother, I clocked fifty-four. Rest easy, though. I promise I won't stay out late." She faced the two men. "Thanks for the delicious meal, Bruce. And Jason, I appreciate the chauffeur service."

He rose. "I'll walk you to your car."

"It isn't necessary."

"Yes, it is."

Hearing his determination, Jenna capitulated. As she pivoted toward the glass door, she glimpsed a satisfied smirk on Abby's face. Vowing to speak to her friend at the next available private moment, she allowed Jason to escort her through the house and down the front sidewalk.

His hand rested at the small of her back. The action had made the fading memory of Chad's touch reach bittersweet proportions. It felt odd for a man other than her husband to perform the small courtesy, yet she enjoyed it more than she thought prudent.

The walk to her car seemed surprisingly short. "I'm glad you decided to join us," he said.

"I am, too." The thought of missing out on such a pleasant evening somehow seemed disturbing. She faltered, uncertain of what to say or do next. It had been a long time—Chad had been her last date—since she'd been in a similar situation.

As if he sensed and understood her hesitation, he grasped her shoulders and gently pulled her toward him until only a hand's-width separated them. A wordless question appeared in his eyes, then, with feather-light care, his mouth touched hers. Time seemed to stand still until he broke away. Weakly, she leaned against the car, her heart racing. She touched her lips, still feeling the light pressure he'd exerted.

"I'd say the evening went very well, wouldn't you?" he murmured. Without waiting for her reply, he stated, "I'll call you tomorrow."

She couldn't answer. Trying to sort out her confusion seemed to take every ounce of concentration she could muster.

"Okay?" he asked, lifting her chin so her eyes met his.

His comment finally registered in her chaotic thoughts. "I don't think you should, Jason," she said gently.

"Why not?"

"I'm happy with my life the way it is."

"I wasn't suggesting a major change. Just dinner. Maybe a movie. We're friends, remember?"

She chewed on her bottom lip. "I can't."

"Can't? Or won't?"

Unable to reply, she lowered her gaze to the hollow of his throat.

"Will you tell me why?"

His intense gaze focused on her like a spotlight. Every dark corner in her being seemed exposed before his eyes. She opened her mouth to deliver her usual vague answer, but her instincts said otherwise. Not only would he see it for the feeble excuse it was, but she couldn't insult his intelligence in such a manner. Jason deserved the truth.

Tears welled in her eyes. She glanced down at her wedding band and twisted it around her finger. "It's your job. It's too dangerous."

"Installing burglar alarms and surveillance cameras is dangerous?" He sounded incredulous.

"Oh, not that." She raised her chin. "It's the rest of the things you do. Can you admit that someone hasn't pulled a gun on you, or that you've been in seedy places trying to get information out of equally seedy characters? That you haven't ever dealt with drug dealers or gun runners or, or. . ." Her mind went blank.

"I've been in a few tight situations," he admitted, "but those have been few and far between."

"Once is all it takes," she said, hating to hear her voice quiver.

"This is about your husband, not me. Isn't it?"

"You're a very special person, Jason. But if anything happened to you, I'm not certain I could cope. I don't want to feel the hurt again."

"Do you trust in God?"

She stared into his eyes. "Yes, but—"

He placed a fingertip on her lips. "Do you believe He has a plan for our lives?"

"Yes, but—"

"Do you trust Him to know what He was doing when He arranged our meeting?"

He'd touched on a truth she'd forgotten. She nodded.

"Then focus on those things instead of your fears." He helped her into the car. "Drive carefully, and I'll call you tomorrow."

As Jenna drove to the hospital, all she could do was pray. Yes, she believed God was in control; He did provide according to his riches and glory.

She and Chad had given up hope for a child of their own, but He had provided a way—a door had opened to adopt a baby. In fact, it would have become a reality if Chad hadn't been killed.

Although she'd been happy for the couple behind them on the waiting list, hearing of their son's arrival a month after her husband's funeral made her feel as if she'd lost two members of her family instead of one.

And so, wouldn't she be foolish to become emotionally tied to another man in a dangerous profession? Hadn't she learned her lesson the first time?

O Lord, help me. Show me the path You want me to take.

four

Jason arrived home in a preoccupied frame of mind. His last moments with Jenna replayed in his mind like a football training film. He understood her fears, but didn't know how to broach the defenses she'd built around them.

He wandered through his house, flicking on light switches to bring a pretense of life to the quiet rooms. The large, two-story frame he'd renovated in his spare time now waited for a loving wife and the pitter-patter of little feet.

He'd thought Suzanne was "The One," but he finally realized he'd never work his way into first, second, or even third place in her life. Her job, her clients, and her perceived social obligations had filled those slots to brimming capacity. To top it off, she'd found no room for a personal relationship with Jesus in her life.

So they'd parted ways. Time marched on and as it did, his dream faded. He didn't particularly *need* a wife. Thanks to his mother's training, Foods I class in high school, and the supermarket's freezer section, he cooked well enough to suit himself. A cleaning lady came on a bi-weekly basis; not because he couldn't handle domestic chores, but because he often didn't have the time. His bachelorhood also had the added attraction of no one nagging him for using too many towels or because he preferred the sports channel to most others.

No, he didn't *need* a wife to cook and clean and take care of him. He wanted one to share his life, his thoughts, his aspirations, and his faith.

It was strang how meeting Jenna had rekindled his wish after all this time. If she was indeed the answer to his prayer, then somehow God would remove the obstacles blocking their path. And while God did His part, Jason would take care of his.

He unbuttoned his shirt, wadded it into a ball, and tossed it into the hamper. There simply had to be a way he could make her understand that every occupation had its inherent risks.

⊱

Jenna drove home, puzzling over her summons to the lab. The staff had been as surprised to see her as Jenna had been to learn there weren't any problems awaiting her attention. According to the shift supervisor, the evening had been strictly routine.

Just as mystifying was the mobile phone operator's insistence that she had not made a mistake—the man had repeated Jenna's name several times.

She shrugged off the incident as she parked her car and grabbed her purse. If the matter was important, he'd call back.

The street lamp on the far corner shed enough light for her to travel up the sidewalk with ease. Nearing the front steps, she stared at the strange shapes on her porch. The shadows were playing tricks on her imagination, she decided.

A step later, she froze. The sight in front of her *was* a trick, but it was the real variety.

Her wide porch was covered with trash.

She slowly climbed the five stairs. Holding her breath against the rank odor, she flinched at the sound of eggshells crunching underneath her shoes. To her relief, the door was still locked. After a quick turn of the key and knob, she reached inside to click on the porch light.

The clutter appeared far worse than she'd expected. Newspapers, broken glass, tin cans, banana peels and coffee grounds covered the concrete. Other things—unrecognizable things—added to the disaster. Her hanging flower baskets had been pulled down and overturned, and the cushions of her lawn chairs had been slashed to ribbons.

Something winged fluttered past her cheek and she brushed at it. Insects drawn by the light joined the company of flies attracted to the rotting food.

Her spirits sank. It would take well over an hour for cleanup, but she couldn't leave this disaster until morning. What a way to end a near-perfect evening!

With a sigh of resignation, she went inside, kicked off her shoes, and padded to the telephone in the kitchen. As she prepared to punch out 911, she stopped. What could the police do? There didn't seem to be any major damage and it would be virtually impossible to find the culprit. With deliberate slowness, she dropped the receiver back into its cradle.

After changing into faded denim shorts and an old bleach-speckled T-shirt, she started to work.

One by one, she mentally reviewed the teens in her neighborhood and, one by one, scratched them off her unofficial list of possible suspects. None of them had ever acted as if they possessed latent destructive tendencies. As far as she knew, no one had any reason to hold a grudge against her.

By the time Jenna had hauled six trash bags to the curb for the morning's sanitation service pickup, she'd decided the culprits had come from another part of town. Although she intended to ask her neighbors if they'd seen or heard anything, her efforts would probably be a futile exercise.

Eighty-year-old Frieda Burns went to bed at nine o'clock and bragged that she could sleep through anything. Maurice and Eloise Marvin were in Oklahoma visiting their grandchildren. The Hill family was on vacation and the next closest house stood vacant. Even so, the people living in her circle deserved a warning.

After liberally hosing down the front porch, she stepped back to survey her work. Although the concrete needed heavy-duty scrubbing in places, it would have to wait until tomorrow.

Tomorrow. Immediately Jason's parting comment came to

mind. *I'll call you tomorrow.*

The water dripping off the railing and puddling in the decorative rocks along the foundation provided a slow background beat to the echoing phrase.

He'd obviously been undaunted by her discouraging remark. Sometime tomorrow—today, she corrected—he'd do exactly as he'd said he would. For a brief moment, excitement rushed through her at the thought of capturing a handsome man's interest. Unbidden, a smile tugged at her mouth.

Seconds later, the thrill faded. She didn't want another man in her life who worked in dangerous situations. Regardless of the sparks flying between Jason and herself, she wanted someone who had a "safe" job—a job that would allow him to come home at night in one piece.

If God didn't send one who met her criteria, it was okay. Her life was just fine the way it was.

ð

Jason strode into St. Anne's Security Department offices the next morning, ready to tackle his assignment with renewed vigor. He also hoped to get a new idea on how to deal with Jenna.

With the full pot of freshly-brewed coffee Bruce's secretary had provided, he and Bruce settled themselves in Jason's temporary headquarters.

"Let's start at the beginning," Jason suggested, removing a handful of files from the cabinet and tossing them onto the desk before he sat down. "Your first case was a Leroy Duncan in the rehab unit."

Bruce nodded. "Mr. Duncan reported fifty dollars were stolen out of his billfold. Now we don't encourage our patients to keep a lot of money, but his five kids paid him a visit on the same day. Unknown to the others, they each gave him ten bucks to use in the vending machines."

Jason glanced through the report. "And he didn't see anyone

enter his room?"

Bruce shook his head.

For the next hour, they discussed the incidents until Jason turned the last page—the one involving Mrs. Harris' ring.

"This is strange," Bruce mused. "Almost every area of the hospital has reported an incident involving our infamous character. He can't be accused of being selective."

Jason leaned forward and began typing into his laptop computer. "I don't know what it is, but something about this just doesn't seem right. It's like I'm missing an important clue, but I can't pinpoint it."

Bruce watched Jason define columns in a grid.

"Let's run through all the places where there's been a theft," Jason said. "We'll cross-reference it by floors and departments."

Fifteen minutes later, he leaned back in his chair and stared at the screen. The inconsistency was obvious, the implications painful.

"What is it?" Bruce asked.

Jason pinched the bridge of his nose before he answered. "There's only one major section where nothing's ever been reported stolen."

Bruce studied the screen again. His puzzled frown suddenly cleared. "The laboratory."

"That's right. Radiology, Pharmacy, Central Supply, and Respiratory Services have all been hit at one time or another."

Jason drummed his fingers on the chair's arm. "There could be a logical reason. The thief may be targeting it next before he moves into the smaller areas, or—"

"Or maybe he works there," Bruce finished.

"Exactly."

Dead silence filled the office.

Bruce folded his arms across his chest. "You sound as if you're leaning toward that theory. You're not considering

Jenna again, are you?"

Jason steepled his fingers and held them to his mouth. He didn't want to suspect the med tech—part of him rebelled at the idea—but the pattern he'd unearthed seemed more than coincidental. "Not really," he prevaricated. "But something is going on in that department. I plan to find out what it is."

"Jenna's not going to like this," Bruce warned.

Jason shrugged. "It can't be helped. We're trying to establish a pattern and look for evidence. To accomplish our goal, we have to question everyone who might be remotely involved."

Bruce nodded. "She'll keep you at arm's length if she thinks you're singling out her or her people. She's very supportive of them, you know."

Jason's jaw clenched. "No joke. She wasn't too happy with me when I asked about her employees the last time. As for keeping me at arm's length, she already does."

"Really? I thought you two got along great."

"We did. But I asked her to dinner, and she refused."

"I'm not surprised, but keep working on her. She'll come around, if you're patient enough to wait." Bruce rose. "Gotta make my rounds. Catch you later."

The morning flew by as Jason updated the two colleagues from his office who were part of his team. After they went their separate ways to carry out their assignments, Jason headed to the cafeteria.

He smiled with satisfaction the moment Jenna appeared ahead of him in the lunch line. How ironic. In spite of her past refusals, he would mark this meal as their third one together. If his luck held, she'd finally say "yes" when he asked for an evening of her time.

In any event, his investigation gave him a legitimate excuse to seek her out.

To his delight, she sat at an unoccupied table for two. Determined to share her company, he hurriedly paid for his meal, then walked to her corner.

"Is this seat taken?" Anticipating her negative response, he placed his tray on the table.

"N. . .no." She cleared her throat, then gestured with her hand. "Be my guest."

Jason pulled out the straight chair and sat down, attributing her nervousness to his surprise approach. He decided to steer the conversation toward light topics. "I see you finally got away."

"Just barely. I'm swamped right now, so I need to get back ASAP. If I hadn't skipped breakfast, I could have bypassed lunch."

Tossing her a look of mock horror, he noted the bowl of fresh strawberries on her tray. "Don't tell me you've forgotten the importance of the first meal of the day." He shook his head. "I'm shocked."

"Sometimes sleep is more important than food."

He paused from unwrapping his ham sandwich to raise one eyebrow. "What time did you get home?"

She cut off one strawberry's leaf. "It was around ten, I guess—not late at all. But someone had dumped garbage all over my porch and it took me until after midnight to clean it up."

"Did you report it to the police?"

She shook her head. As if sensing his disapproval, she defended herself. "I didn't find any real damage, so I figured it was a waste of time. I'm sure it was only a teenage prank. I just happened to be chosen as the lucky homeowner."

"Vandalism is a crime, too."

"I realize that, and maybe I should have called the authorities, but I was tired. Besides, the mess was merely a nuisance. Don't worry, though," she added, "if it happens again, I'll notify someone. I promise."

Satisfied by her assurance, he let the matter drop. "So what are you doing this evening?"

"After I scrub my porch again, I have an early date with my bed."

"Can I interest you in supper first? I promise to get you home before dark."

"Jason, like I said last night, I don't want to get involved with—"

"—people in dangerous jobs," he finished for her. "But I'm talking a simple supper between friends. You wouldn't turn down a meal if Bruce or Abby invited you, would you?"

Her troubled expression reflected the accuracy of his statement. He sensed her indecision.

She shook her head. "Sorry, but I can't tonight. My trip to the grocery store won't wait and neither will my porch. Besides, I'm really beat."

Knowing he'd see her frequently in the days ahead, he decided not to press. "I understand. You do look tired. Some other evening. Be prepared, though. I will ask again." He softened his warning with a lopsided grin.

"I thought you would," she mumbled. Her voice grew stronger. "You've heard about my day; how's yours been? Any more ideas about the thief?"

Following her abrupt change of subject, he shook his head and swallowed before answering. "Not really." Until proven, his suspicions were just that—suspicions.

"Some of the employees are calling him 'the ghost'."

"An apt name, I suppose."

"I'll say. Items disappear from plain sight without a trace—no witnesses, no fingerprints. Like a ghost. Spooky, isn't it?" She shivered. "Of course, Payce would have a coronary if this hit the papers."

"I'm sure he would," Jason remarked dryly. "Believe me, this isn't the work of a ghost. He's pure flesh and blood and we'll find him. Or her," he tacked on. "You can count on it."

By the time everyone in Jenna's department had taken a lunch break, the workload had slowed to a more manageable level. Jenna took advantage of the situation to meet Abby for a quick conference. Intercepting her colleague in the hospital's outpatient clinic lab, she cut to the heart of the matter preying on her mind.

"Abby, what did you or Bruce tell Jason about me?" she demanded.

The blonde smiled and pulled her friend into the nearest corner to talk semi-privately. "We didn't tell him you were a prison escapee or anything. Why? What's wrong?"

"Everything. . .nothing. . .I don't know." Agitated, Jenna ran her hand through her curls.

"Start at the beginning," Abby demanded, a glimmer of a smile crossing her lips. She leaned against the counter, her hands deep in the pockets of her lab coat.

"I ate lunch with Jason today." At this news Abby raised one eyebrow. "And he invited me to supper tonight."

"That certainly is cause for alarm," Abby said with a straight face. "Are you going?"

"No, but. . ."

"Why not? He obviously likes you or he wouldn't be giving you a second thought." Abby raised her hands to stop her friend from speaking. "So what's the problem? He seems like a very nice guy."

"He is, but—"

"But what?"

Jenna felt her shoulders slump. "I don't know what to do or what to think. I put my life in order after Chad died, and now Jason walks in and turns it all topsy-turvy."

"God gives wisdom freely—all you have to do is ask for it. Then, receive His guidance by faith." Abby touched Jenna's arm. "God may intend for you to do something other than devote yourself to your career. If Jason is part of that plan—"

"But he could get himself killed," Jenna wailed.

Abby waved away the comment. "Accidents happen in every job; no occupation is immune. While some professions are riskier than others, bad things happen to everyone.

"Besides, fear isn't from God," she continued. "Maybe He's leading you into a situation where you'll have to trust in Him and set aside your preconceived ideas. Only you can answer that. Now, I'm not saying Jason is *the* right man for you, but if he is, you don't want to miss out on God's best, do you?"

Jenna slowly shook her head and twisted a loose thread on a button. "I'm only looking ahead, trying to avoid a problem before it develops."

"You mentioned how you'd put your life in order. Maybe you should let God be in charge for a change."

Jenna scraped her teeth along her bottom lip. Abby's eyes took on a knowing gleam. "He's special, isn't he?"

Jenna nodded.

Abby gave her a hug. "Go home and get a good night's sleep. Believe me, everything will be clearer in the morning."

"I suppose."

"It will. You gave me that prescription when I had my own problems and it worked. It's only appropriate for you to take a dose of the same medicine."

The telephone interrupted their conversation and Abby groaned. "No doubt it's Dr. Kirkman wanting another strep screen. We must be running a special this week. Don't forget—everything will work out, trust me. By the way, can you take these samples with you? The courier won't stop by for at least an hour."

"No problem." Jenna picked up the carryall containing tubes of blood and returned to the lab.

Sam stopped her just as she delivered Abby's samples to the specimen receiving area. "The security fellow—Mr. Daly—is waiting in Masters' office."

"Did he say what he wanted?" she asked, hoping for a clue pertaining to the purpose of his visit.

Sam shook his head.

"Okay." Jenna strode toward her boss's sanctum with some trepidation. This couldn't be a social call since they'd just shared lunch. Official business came to mind, a thought she didn't find reassuring.

She entered the room and saw Jason studying the plaques and certificates on the wall. "This is a surprise. If I'd known you were coming, I'd have saved my errand until later."

He turned to greet her. "No problem. The secretary said you'd be back any time, so I waited."

Comforted by his non-urgent tone, her worries faded. She sat down and he followed suit. "What can I do for you?"

"My staff and I will be in your section for the next few days. We're reviewing areas that might need closed-circuit monitoring and, with your permission, we hope to interview your employees."

Getting her permission was a mere formality; George Payce had already sent notices out for hospital personnel to cooperate. Although she appreciated Jason's thoughtfulness, she was disheartened to learn of his intent to begin his probe in her area.

She crossed her arms. "I thought you weren't limiting your search to this department."

"I'm not. I've divided my team so we'll be covering several areas of the hospital at once."

"Oh." Her gaze fell and she tugged on the collar of her lab jacket. He hadn't ended up in her section by accident; she was sure of it. At the same time, she wondered if she should be concerned or flattered.

"We'll concentrate on your floor plan today and tomorrow in order to determine if your security measures are adequate," he said. "Then I'll visit with you to get the basic background information on your staff."

"Okay."

"You have about a hundred employees so it will take a while. Probably a week to ten days."

"I see." She wondered how she'd manage to keep her relationship with him on a platonic basis for that length of time. In spite of her reservations, she was drawn to him and she freely admitted it. It was almost like staring at a box of rich, gooey chocolates—she wanted to taste and experience the flavor, but she didn't want to pay the price of gaining weight.

She toyed with a pencil lying on the desk. "I'll help whenever I can, but my time isn't my own since John is on vacation."

"I understand. Any spare moment you can give me will be appreciated."

A thought suddenly occurred to her. The sooner she answered his questions, the sooner he'd move to the next department. Temptation would be out of reach.

She grasped at the obvious solution. With some creative juggling, her idea would work. On the other hand, he seemed content to fit himself into her hectic schedule, a surprising phenomenon for a person whose objective was to solve St. Anne's mystery at the earliest opportunity.

"One of my associates should be here shortly and then we'll get started."

Just as Jason finished speaking, Sam appeared in the doorway with another gentleman wearing a tailored navy suit. Jason introduced Gary Burrows before the two began their self-guided tour. Meanwhile, Jenna and her colleague returned to work.

For the next hour, she did her best to ignore Jason's presence and achieved marginal success. But after he left at three o'clock, she attributed her letdown feeling to tiredness.

Heading to the parking lot at three-thirty, she mentally

reviewed her evening. A well-deserved nap sounded much better than a trip to the grocery store, but her shopping expedition couldn't be postponed. She'd squeezed the last bit of toothpaste out of the tube this morning and her last cup of milk had soured.

Her second order of business was a long, hot shower, followed by a soft, cool bed.

The inside of her car felt like the inside of a hot oven. She rolled down the window, removed her cardboard sun guard with its "Save the Baby Humans, Stop Abortion" message from the windshield, then turned the ignition key.

Total silence greeted her. *Of all days for my car to go on strike!* Although she performed basic maintenance chores like checking fluid levels and the air filter, anything more than that fell beyond her expertise. After several tries, she hopped out to raise the hood. Taking care to keep from burning her hand on the hot metal, she hoped the problem would be glaringly obvious.

It was.

Her battery was missing.

five

I don't believe this, she thought, staring at the two cables hanging in the empty space. *Lord, I could use some help right now.*

"Having trouble?"

The unexpected sound of a male voice near her ear made her jump, but Jason's presence was extremely reassuring. She wouldn't have to deal with her dilemma alone.

"Someone has stolen my battery. Can you believe it?" She pointed to the empty space.

Jason handed her the coat he'd slung over one shoulder. While he studied the latch, he asked, "Do you lock your car?"

"Always. So how could they raise the hood?"

"I don't see any scratch marks, so they probably used a shim to open the door. Then they pulled the hood release. In any case, we should report this. I'll call security."

"Thanks." To be honest, she liked it when he'd said "we." After Chad had died, she'd learned to deal with problems involving home maintenance and car repair, but she couldn't deny her relief at having Jason take charge.

He reappeared a few minutes later. "I notified the police. We shouldn't have long to wait," he said, stripping off his tie and unbuttoning his top shirt button. "I'll stay if you want me to."

Although she wanted to give an emphatic "yes," she settled for "I'd hate to interfere with your evening."

He rubbed at the beads of perspiration on his forehead. "I'd hoped to convince you to join me for supper, so I didn't make any plans. After we handle all the details, I'll get your car running again."

"I'd appreciate it."

The police officer who'd arrived was sympathetic, but not hopeful about finding the guilty party. A report would be filed and a detective would contact her if they needed further information. By the time he left the scene, both physical and mental exhaustion threatened to overtake her. She stifled a yawn. The long days and short nights of the past week were taking their toll.

Jason glanced at his watch. "It's only five o'clock. Why don't I take you home, let you rest, and then we can deal with your car later? It won't be going anywhere."

She smiled at his dry humor. "Your offer is tempting, but—"

"In the meantime, I'll scout out the sales. As Ben Franklin said, 'a penny saved, is a penny earned'."

"I'm too hot and tired to argue. We'll do it your way."

Jason fought the urge to shout out a war whoop and settled instead for an ear-to-ear smile. By the time he'd installed himself behind the wheel of his sports-utility vehicle, he'd erased all traces of satisfaction off his face.

Jenna tilted her head back and closed her eyes.

"Rough day?" he asked.

"Rough week. Thank goodness tomorrow is Friday."

She fell silent and he used the ten-minute drive to her house to think. Why would someone go to the trouble to steal a battery and nothing else? The policeman wasn't particularly helpful, either, attributing the incident to an isolated prank. Although Jason was inclined to agree, it seemed too coincidental for her to be victimized twice in two days.

As he parked next to the curb, Jenna opened her eyes and unfastened her seat belt. "Thanks again for the lift."

"My pleasure. I'll see you inside." At her protest, he added, "Don't argue. I insist."

The ambient temperature in her home was a welcome respite to the outdoor heat. Pointing toward the bedroom, he said tenderly, "Go. I'll take care of your car."

"But. . ."

He placed a finger on her lips. "Take a nap. I'll see you later."

Two hours later, he returned to her house. He knocked at the door but, receiving no answer, surmised she was still asleep. Taking advantage of the daylight, he skirted the house in search of clues to the vandals' identities.

His efforts fruitless, he decided to wash down the porch for her. The green garden hose lay curled on the ground, already hooked to the outdoor faucet. With a few squeaky turns of the knob, he was in business.

By the time he'd finished, a tousle-haired Jenna, wearing casual clothes, stepped outside. "I thought I heard water running. You didn't have to do that," she chided, her voice husky.

"I know, but I wanted to help."

She finger-combed her curls. "I'll be ready to leave in a few minutes."

A pizza delivery truck stopped at the curb. Jason dug out his billfold. "Supper has arrived, so if you don't mind, I'd rather eat first."

He paid for the order, then headed straight for the kitchen. "Hungry?" he asked, sliding the warm box onto the table.

Jenna dropped ice into two glasses and poured lemonade over the cubes. "You bet. Tell me something, though. Why is it that whenever we're together, we're always eating or talking about it?"

He grinned. "Would you believe I hate to dine alone?"

"Maybe."

"It's true. Good company helps the digestion."

She looked dubious. "Are you sure?"

"Of course. When a person is relaxed and enjoying him or herself, the stomach functions better. If you're tense, so's your stomach and the food just sits there."

"Makes sense," she mused. "Although I'd never thought about it."

"Even the Bible says so. Verses in Proverbs—chapters fifteen and seventeen, to be exact—mention the very subject."

"I might have known you'd memorize Scriptures that deal with food."

He faked an aggrieved tone. "Hey, now. I have a few other verses tucked away for use. Want to hear 'em?"

She laughed. "Maybe later. Right now, I'd rather eat."

"A woman after my own heart."

"You took a quite chance ordering pizza. What if I didn't like it?"

"Not like pizza?" He pretended outrage. "That's absolutely un-American." He stopped to wash his hands before serving the food. "Actually, after some simple deductive reasoning, I knew it was a safe choice."

She accepted a plate holding two thin-crusted slices covered with all of the toppings. "Really?"

"The empty box near your trash was a good clue."

"Excellent, Mr. Holmes, but did you find a battery?"

He swallowed, nodding. "I found a good sale, too."

"I should have told you to go ahead and buy one. Batteries are all the same to me."

He smiled. "I thought about it, but I didn't want to offend you in case you preferred to make the final decision." Her answer showed him another side to her character. Although she wasn't helpless, and he agreed women shouldn't be, she obviously wouldn't feel threatened by a man's act of consideration.

After the pizza, followed by strawberries for dessert, they were on their way to the department store where batteries were on sale. With Jenna's purchase on the back seat floor, Jason drove past a supermarket. "Didn't you need groceries? I'm out of a few things, myself."

"I can wait for another time."

"We're already here, so why bother?" Within minutes, they were pushing shopping carts down the aisles.

At the checkout lanes, Jason compared their purchases. Sh
had chosen whole-grain bread, a wide assortment of fresh veg
etables, skim milk, and chicken, not to mention a tube of tootl
paste.

On the other hand, he had filled his cart with several froze
entrees, a head of lettuce, chocolate ice cream, several package
of cookies, bacon, and a dozen eggs. To his credit, he also ha
low-fat cottage cheese and a large bunch of grapes. A cardboal
carton of chocolate milk stood next to a gallon of two-percel
white milk.

"How can you drink all that?"

The wonderment in her voice made him grin. "Have t
keep the dairy farmers in business, you know."

The clerk rang up his purchases after hers and Jason couldn
resist commenting on Jenna's expression. "I can tell you're
conscientious chemist."

"Oh?"

"Uh huh. You're adding up fat grams and cholesterol col
tent."

Her face took on a rosy hue. "I am not. Well, maybe."

As they loaded their groceries into the back of his vehicle,
woman who seemed vaguely familiar to Jason pulled into th
empty parking stall next to them.

"Hello, there," she called out to Jenna, her eyes bright wit
interest. "Grocery shopping?"

"You bet," Jen replied, her smile forced. "Gotta run. See yo
tomorrow, Marian," she added, climbing into the four-wheele
drive vehicle.

Jason started the engine. "I'm not in any hurry. You coul
have visited for a while."

Jenna shook her head. "Once Marian starts talking, it'
impossible to get away. Besides, she's the biggest gossip in m
department. By morning there won't be a soul who doesn
know we've been together. I should have told her that you wel

only giving me a lift, though. Now she'll dream up some ridiculous story to spread."

"Afraid of a little gossip?"

She stared at him. "Doesn't it bother you?"

"No. Something juicier always attracts the grapevine's attention, so I don't worry about it."

"I suppose." She wasn't naive enough to believe she'd never been the subject of someone's speculation, but being a private person, she hated the idea of rumors floating around. She'd had enough of those after Chad's death to last a lifetime.

Deep in her thoughts, she didn't notice they'd arrived at the hospital until Jason parked beside her car. Within minutes, he'd installed her battery.

"Now try it," he said.

The engine started with a purr.

He dropped the hood with a bang and brushed his hands together. "I'll follow you home. Just leave the groceries for now. No point in moving things unnecessarily."

"Only if you're sure you don't mind the extra stop."

"Not at all. What are friends for?"

Could she and Jason be friends in the same way Bruce was her friend? She doubted it. The air seemed charged and filled with sparks whenever Jason was nearby.

It wasn't long before four brown paper sacks stood in a row on her kitchen countertop. Suddenly hating to end their time together, Jenna offered him a glass of iced tea.

"It's getting late. I'll take a rain check, though."

She accompanied him to the curb. "Thanks again for your help," she called out, watching as he opened the door and moved to climb inside.

A sudden slam caught her by surprise, as did his purposeful approach. "Forget something?" she asked.

"Yes, I did." He flung his arms around her, bent his head and kissed her gently. Locusts provided the background music—a summertime symphony.

"I'm developing quite a taste for strawberries," he said after a moment.

Her senses were still scrambled. "Oh?"

He grinned. "Afraid so."

"Thanks again for everything." She heard her own breathlessness.

"Everything?"

Her face warmed, knowing he referred to their kiss. Her answer was faint. "Yes."

He stroked her cheek. "My pleasure."

❧

The vehicle's red tail lights winked in the growing darkness. Jenna lifted her hand in farewell, strangely bereft at Jason's departure.

Forcing herself to snap out of her mood, she hurried inside. She restocked her cupboards and refrigerator by rote, noticing how quiet the house seemed now that she was alone. Funny thing, she'd never noticed it before. Did it mean she was finally ready to let someone special come into her life? Was Jason that someone special?

She clicked on the radio to catch a Christian broadcast, but her mind wandered. She pictured Jason helping around the house with a toddler hanging on his leg, a baby perched on his arm. She saw herself preparing a meal, receiving a "Honey, I'm home" kiss. The warm fuzzy feeling spreading through her made her smile.

The dream faded, chased into oblivion. The chances of that particular fantasy coming true were infinitesimal, with or without Jason. A familiar heartache began to grow and she resorted to the only cure she knew.

"Thank You, Heavenly Father, for sending Jason when I needed him," she prayed aloud. "But now I need Your wisdom and guidance more than ever. I need to know if You want

Jason in my life. I know Your Word says that You haven't given us a spirit of fear, but I am fearful. I don't want to lose someone I care about like I lost Chad. Forgive me for worrying, and help me to see my situation clearly. I ask this in Jesus' name."

&

"Did you hear about Jenna's car?" Bruce asked Jason the next morning.

Jason spooned creamer into his mug of black coffee. "I happened to be in the parking lot when she discovered she had a problem. I turned it in."

"Do the police have any clues?"

"Not a one. Has anything like this happened before?"

Bruce shook his head. "We've had cameras, tools, and purses stolen out of vehicles, but never actual car parts."

Jason dropped some crushed ice into his drink and stirred. "Did you know vandals trashed her house the other night?"

"No, I didn't."

"Another interesting coincidence. Jenna seems to have attracted the attention of the local criminal element."

"What do we do?"

Jason shrugged. "Keep watching and waiting. It wouldn't hurt to keep an eye on her."

Bruce sported a knowing smile. "Not exactly unpleasant duty for you, is it?"

"Can't say that it is, buddy. Hey, didn't you have a date last night with Lila?"

"Lydia," Bruce corrected. "Lydia Austin. It went well too; we got along great. It's hard finding the time to be together, though."

"Can't she transfer to another shift?"

"She probably could, but I think she needs the extra income from the pay differential. Her parents are dead and she's helping her younger sister with her expenses at Wichita State." The sandy-haired security director let out a sigh. "She helps out a brother, too, but she doesn't say much about him. I gather he's got his own problems."

Jason gulped down his coffee. "Hope it works out for you. In the meantime, I'm off to the lab. I'll check in around noon."

With that, he strode out of the office and into the main corridor, humming to himself.

In spite of yesterday's unfortunate circumstances, he was certain Jenna had enjoyed her evening. Now he was anxious to see if some of the walls she'd built around herself had tumbled.

He ambled toward her desk at the same time she glanced in his direction. Her countenance lit up like the bright summer sun and he counted her enthusiasm as a positive sign. Maybe it was his imagination, but her whole demeanor seemed more relaxed.

His spirits lifted. He never thought he'd be thankful for a stolen battery, but he was. That one incident had brought about a turning point in their relationship.

"Good morning," she said.

He smiled. "As my mother often told us, 'You look bright-eyed and bushy-tailed, today'."

The color in her face heightened. "Thanks. I had a good night's sleep, among other things."

It seemed presumptuous to explain her newfound peace concerning their budding relationship, nor did she want to draw attention to the now-bare ring finger on her left hand.

She changed the subject. "We'll use John's office. It's a little more private."

"Sounds fine." He stepped aside and motioned her ahead. At her urging, he accepted John's comfortably padded executive chair.

"Would you like coffee or tea?" she asked.

Jason shook his head. "Just had a cup. Maybe later."

He reached into his shirt pocket and retrieved a black book

and a gold pen. His long fingers twisted the barrel, and she forced the memory of his warm touch into the background. *Acting like a teenager at my age!*

"Where would you like to begin?" she asked in a businesslike tone, sitting between him and the drawer containing personnel records.

He opened his notes. "Human Resources supplied me with the basics. I'd like some insight into your people's character, things about them that may never enter into an evaluation."

"I've only been here a little over six months. I don't know most of them very well," she warned.

"Do the best you can. We'll start alphabetically so I don't miss anyone."

By the time noon arrived, they had only progressed to the H's. "I'm ready for a break. How about you?" he asked.

"Me, too."

"Sorry to interrupt, Jenna," Margery said from the doorway. "We're having problems with Pete."

It took a second for Jenna to redirect her thoughts. To her disappointment, her other responsibilities had intruded. Yet, it couldn't be helped.

She sighed. "I'll be right there."

"Staff trouble?" he asked.

She chuckled. "Pete is the nickname of our profiling instrument. It's temperamental and needs to be replaced."

The furrows between his eyebrows disappeared. "Then while you're busy, I'll take care of other business."

A short time later, she retraced her steps to John's office and relayed bad news.

"I'm sorry," she said. "We'll have to work on your project another time. I'll be tied up for the rest of the day." This time she didn't bother to hide her frustration. She did, however, feel a little better to see his smile dim. He was obviously just as unhappy about the turn of events.

"I understand. Duty comes first," he told her. "But if it's okay, I'll check with you later in case the situation changes."

"Please do."

The afternoon wore on while Jenna and Margery performed repairs. Each time they thought the problem was resolved, the instrument seemed to develop another glitch. Malfunctioning telephones added to Jenna's frustration. The static had gotten so loud, she could hardly hear the party speaking at the other end.

Jason's call became her only bright spot. To her regret, however, she was still unavailable.

By seven o'clock—nearly four hours past her shift—she'd replaced a multitude of parts and miles of tubing. "I'm going to the coffee shop for a sandwich," she informed one of the afternoon chemistry techs as she massaged the kinks in her neck. "We'll know by the time I get back if our repair job worked."

Taking the current issue of a professional journal with her, she ordered a grilled cheese and a pink lemonade.

"We've got fresh pie this evening," Bev, the waitress, coaxed. "Cherry, apple, banana cream, and chocolate meringue."

"No, thanks."

"Oh yeah. And strawberry-rhubarb."

"In that case, I'll have a piece. Anything with strawberries in it has to be good."

Jenna ate hastily, but savored each bite of her dessert. Back in the lab thirty minutes later, she was delighted to hear good news. "Pete" seemed to be working fine, and she could finally go home.

On the home front, however, the situation wasn't as encouraging.

six

Frieda Burns hobbled down the sidewalk, leaning heavily on her cane. "I'm glad you're home, Jenna, dear. I came outside to water my marigolds when I glanced over and saw what someone had done to your house. I'm appalled. Simply appalled."

Jenna couldn't reply. Numb from shock and disbelief, she felt as if she were living a nightmare. She stumbled closer for a better look.

Black and red blotches of paint marred the white siding. Even the navy-blue window trim and shutters hadn't escaped the vandals' attention.

"This is terrible. Just terrible." Frieda thumped her cane on the sidewalk for emphasis. "This has always been such a safe neighborhood, too."

A lump formed in Jenna's throat. What was happening here? In spite of the heat, she felt chilled, lightheaded, and, somehow, violated.

"You'd better sit down, honey. You don't look so good."

Jenna complied, sinking onto the top step. A police car with its lights flashing rounded the corner and braked at the curb.

"I took the liberty of calling 911," Frieda stated. "Hope you don't mind."

"Thanks." Jenna rose as the officer approached. Although several years had passed since a uniformed deputy had brought the news of her husband's death, seeing this one stride toward her resurrected the memory—and the pain—in vivid detail.

The blond patrolman in his mid-twenties shook his head

and whistled as he stared at the damage. "Your visitors left their mark."

"No joke."

Jenna introduced Frieda, then herself, while Officer Malone pulled a small notepad from his left breast pocket.

He clicked his pen and poised his hand over a blank page. "Tell me what you know."

Frieda gave her statement which, unfortunately, was brief since she hadn't seen or heard anything.

"Let's see what we can find," he said, moving away to circle the house.

Luckily, only the front side had been marred. Even so, Jenna knew how hard she'd worked to paint her home last fall. Trying to cover red and black would make the task more difficult. Her fury simmered.

"Have there been any other incidents, either here or in the neighborhood?" Malone asked.

"My front porch was trashed a few nights ago, too," Jenna said, describing the scene. "There's a vacant house across the street and another neighbor is out of town. It doesn't make sense for someone to bother mine."

"Not all criminals are smart."

"I also had my car battery stolen while I was at work," she added.

He stopped writing to stare at her. "Do you have any enemies, Mrs. Carlson?"

"None that I'm aware of."

He jotted down the details before he stuffed the pad into his pocket.

"Now what happens?" Jenna asked.

"I'll file a report, question your neighbors and some of the kids we encounter. Unfortunately, unless they're caught in the act or we find a witness, we may never identify the responsible party. Once in a while we run across someone with a guilty conscience, but I wouldn't count on it."

"Is this the work of a gang?" Frieda asked.

"I really can't say," Malone replied. "But if I were you, I'd call my insurance agent." With that parting comment, he left.

"Will you be all right, my dear?" Frieda asked.

Jenna squared her shoulders and forced a smile. "Sure. I'll follow Malone's advice and let the insurance company handle it. Go on home."

"If you need me for anything, promise you'll call."

"I will."

Jenna went inside. Still reeling from shock, she pulled on the inner strength that saw her through her husband's death. A phone call to her insurance agent yielded disappointing news.

"I'll send an adjuster out first thing in the morning," the man said. "But if there isn't any structural damage, the cost of repainting may not exceed your deductible. Regardless, I'll start the paperwork."

"Thanks." Jenna broke the connection. Next, she dialed Abby's phone number and left a brief message on the answering machine for either her or Bruce to call.

A familiar ache began to build between her shoulder blades. If only someone had been available to share this burden with her.

"Dear God," she prayed. "I know You don't give us more than we can bear, but I'm really at my limit. Nothing is hidden from Your eyes, so guide the police to the guilty party, and help me not to be unforgiving toward those responsible. I ask too, for Your protection of my home and my property. In Jesus' name. Amen."

Although she felt secure with her divine protection, she also needed to do her part. One certainly didn't court danger unnecessarily.

She could only think of one deterrent. Although she had no idea how effective it was, she decided to try it.

For the first time in her life, she slept with the lights on.

❧

"Nothing like this has ever happened to me," one waitress said, wringing her hands. "My evaluation is due in a few days. This won't affect my raise, will it?"

"Oh, my. I never thought of that," the other said.

Standing in the hospital coffee shop near eleven P.M., Jason exchanged a look of frustration with Bruce. The two college-aged waitresses were too rattled by their recent discovery to give a coherent statement. Too bad they hadn't noticed their loss earlier.

While Bruce stood ready to document the incident, Jason shifted his weight to widen his stance. He spoke to the red-haired woman who seemed to be the one in charge. "Tell us everything you remember."

"Stella and I were swamped tonight," Bev said. "We usually take part of the money out of the register after the supper crowd, put it in the bank bag, and lock it in the cabinet. When I noticed the big bills were gone, I thought Stella had taken care of it."

"I thought the same thing," Stella chimed in, nodding for emphasis. "I locked the doors over there—I always do. Anyways, after that, I looked in the cash register and the only money left was the little bills and some change. Then I saw the bank bag was empty. I said something to Bev and that's when we figured we got robbed."

"Maybe you just *think* you took in more money than you actually did." Bruce suggested.

Bev shook her head emphatically. "Oh no, sir. I made change for a bunch of twenties—it was payday today, you know—and there's only one in the drawer now."

"Speaking of which, you're sure you didn't leave the drawer open at some point?"

Both Stella and Bev appeared affronted. "Absolutely not.

We're not *that* careless."

Jason tried again. "Did anyone horse around or ask any questions about the register?"

They shook their heads.

"Who were your customers?" Bruce asked.

Both girls named several regulars. "A couple of student nurses came in around nine," Stella reported. "But I don't know who they are because I've never seen them before."

"Did anyone look out of place or uncomfortable?" Jason asked. When the women looked blank, he continued. "Did anyone do or say anything that stands out in your mind?"

"Two guys from the maintenance department talked about getting tattoos," Stella added helpfully.

Bruce covered his mouth and cleared his throat in an obvious attempt to hide his amusement.

"Anything else?" prompted Jason.

"To be honest, I was too busy to notice. After I cut a piece of strawberry-rhubarb pie for the lady from the lab, everything is just a blur," Bev admitted.

Jason's attention perked. "Someone from the lab stopped in?"

Bev nodded. "Yeah. She came by herself and read a magazine. I guess it was around seven. It was sort of slow then."

"Do you remember her name?" Bruce asked.

"No," Bev replied, "but she has curly brown hair. I could tell she loves strawberries because she didn't want any pie until I mentioned the strawberry-rhubarb."

Jason's heart pounded and he refrained from looking at his partner. The woman Bev described had to be Jenna.

"Okay, you can go," he said. "If we need more information, we'll be in touch."

The two girls left and the men approached the cook, a heavy-set woman with steel-gray hair, who delivered her statement without any attempt at civility.

"I didn' see nuthing, I didn' hear nuthing, and I didn' do

nuthing 'cept run my legs off tonight," Mrs. Meadows declared, her large bosom heaving. "My kitchen helper called in sick and I ended up doin' her job plus my own. All's I saw tonight was the orders Bev and Stella tacked up for me to cook. Now, can I go home? My corns are killing me. I jist don' understand how they 'spect me to handle that entire kitchen by myself."

Convinced she couldn't add anything to Bev and Stella's story and afraid she'd continue her diatribe on the unfairness of her supervisor and life in general, Jason sent the woman on her way.

Later, in the privacy of Bruce's office, Jason asked, "How much was taken?"

"Assuming this payday ran like all the others, the supervisor guessed between eight and eleven hundred dollars."

"Fingerprints?"

Bruce shook his head. "Too many people have been in that cash register."

"First thing Monday, we'll track down the people Stella and Bev mentioned. Maybe one of them saw something."

"What about Jenna?"

"I'll get in touch with her tomorrow." Jason glanced at his watch. "Hey, aren't you supposed to meet Lydia soon?"

Bruce grinned. "In fifteen minutes, to be exact."

Jason clapped him on the back. "Go ahead. We've done all we can, for now."

It was a shame it was so late, he thought as he hopped into his vehicle. He was anxious to talk to Jenna.

❧

Jenna was anxious to talk to Jason.

She climbed the aluminum stepladder, armed with all the tools necessary to scrape off the paint. For the past twelve hours, her thoughts dwelled on ways to prevent vandals from attacking her home. True, she had nothing of real value to require an elaborate security system, but there had to be something she could do to deter these hellions.

She yawned and nearly lost her balance. As she grabbed a rung, her tools fell onto the ground. With a frustrated sigh, she backed down the ladder and retrieved the chisel and hand-sander. Her eyes felt as gritty as sandpaper and every muscle ached.

At three A.M. she'd decided to shut off most of the lights. Not only couldn't she sleep, but if the vandals had attacked her home in broad daylight, lights wouldn't stop them either. She turned up the volume of her Christian music before mounting the ladder once again.

The cool morning slowly gave way to the heat. Wiping the sweat from her brow, she drained her insulated mug of ice water and stood back to survey her handiwork. One-half of the front side was scraped down to the bare wood siding and ready for a primer coat. At least she was making progress.

A door slammed behind her and she inwardly groaned. She didn't feel like explaining the situation to another curious neighbor, nor was she in the mood to listen to someone's assessment of today's youth. Intending to keep the conversation short, she turned to greet her latest visitor. Recognizing her guest, however, she dismissed her plan as quickly as it had been made.

Dressed in faded denim shorts, a jade-and-purple golf shirt, and running shoes, Jason cut across the grass carrying a small white paper sack.

His gaze was fixed directly on her home. "I'd ask what happened, but it's fairly obvious."

"Isn't it, though?" she agreed, mentally comparing her hot, sweaty, wilted daisy look to his fresh, perky one. "The sad thing is, I repainted everything last fall. I hadn't planned to redo it so soon."

"Were there any signs of entry at the windows?"

She shook her head.

After placing the bag on the top step, he strode past the ladder to the nearest ground-floor window and scrutinized the casing. Methodically, he worked his way around the entire structure with Jenna at his heels like an adoring puppy.

He didn't speak until he'd circled the house. "Only the street side appears damaged. They obviously wanted you to see the destruction right away."

"I certainly did," Jenna answered in disgust. "It takes a warped mind to dump garbage on a person's porch and spray paint her house. I'd like some professional advice on how to prevent this from happening again." She swallowed hard, hoping he hadn't heard the catch in her voice.

"I'd recommend motion detector lights."

"Okay, but what about during the daytime?"

Jason didn't hesitate. "A dog."

"You're probably right, but I would hate to leave an animal chained to the porch all day."

"Install a fence."

The expense seemed astronomical. "I'll think about it."

"I could wire your windows with an alarm, but it doesn't appear they're interested in getting inside."

"That's some consolation." Overwhelmed by his suggestions, she changed the subject. "So, what brings you to my proverbial neck of the woods?"

He pointed to the white bag. "It's a little late in the morning, but I brought breakfast. Fresh donuts, to be exact."

"Great. I've been up since dawn and I could use a break." She led the way into her kitchen.

"Couldn't sleep?"

She poured two large glasses of chilled orange juice. "No, I couldn't. I also wanted to get as much done as possible before the heat got unbearable." She pulled a jelly donut from the sack. "Ummmm, strawberry."

He grinned. "I thought you'd like it." Taking a sugary twist for himself, he casually mentioned, "St. Anne's had another robbery yesterday."

"No kidding? Where?"

"The coffee shop. Sometime between seven and ten last night."

"Really? I stopped there for a sandwich before I came home from work."

"I know."

His matter-of-fact tone and impassive expression sent a shiver of fear coursing down her spine. The pastry in her stomach seemed to turn into a cement block.

"Are you accusing me?" she asked.

"No, but I'd like to ask you a few questions."

She held herself tense. "Like what?"

"Did you see or recognize anyone while you were there?"

She chewed on her lip and felt an ache begin between her eyes. "Two candy-stripers were leaving as I walked in, and I think there were a couple of EMT firemen. I don't remember if they were still there when I left or not."

"Did you see anything unusual with the cash register? Did Bev leave the drawer open? Was there a lot of money inside?"

"I didn't look," she snapped, her emotions threatening to erupt. "I only paid attention to the change she gave me for my five-dollar bill."

She jumped to her feet, her chair scraping the floor. With uncharacteristic abruptness, she said, "I have to get back to work now."

Brushing at the tears pooling in her eyes, she stomped through the kitchen and into the living room. The destruction of her property had been stressful enough without Jason's third-degree. Just because he'd found one ring on her desk, would he link her to every incident at the hospital? After all their time together, he should know her by now. Or was he using her to further his investigation? *O Lord, why has my life spun out of control?*

Jason caught up with her just as she twisted the knob. He reached around her to press his palms against the door, effectively trapping her in his embrace at the same time. "I didn' mean to upset you," he murmured in her ear. "But Bruce and have to question everyone who was or might be connected to the scene of the crime."

"Fine. You've done your job and now you can go. But before you do, I want to know one thing." She turned to face him. "Are you going to suspect me every time something happens at St. Anne's?"

He lowered his hands to his side. "I'm being paid to suspect everyone. It's my job," he said quietly.

Unable to help herself, she pressed on. His reply might be painful, but she needed to hear it. "I'd like an honest answer. Is this why you're spending so much time with me? Are you trying to prove I'm guilty?"

His hazel gaze met hers unwaveringly. "No. Absolutely not."

"I'm not sure I believe you."

"It's the truth." His answer seemed heartfelt and sounded most emphatic.

She drew a shaky breath as she swiped her tear-filled eyes.

He tugged her into his embrace. Near the breaking point she didn't resist. "You know what I think?"

Jenna rested her cheek against his chest. "No, what?"

"You need to get away."

"Yeah, right."

"I'm serious," he insisted. "I'm driving home to Hutchinson tomorrow, for my nephew's birthday. Why don't you come along?"

She lifted her head. "I can't. I have to finish repainting."

"I'll help you scrape and with any luck, we'll brush on the primer coat this evening."

"You don't have to do this."

"I may not have to, but I want to. So, what do you say?"

What will it hurt? she wondered. As much as she accomplished by herself, the two of them working together would be done in half the time. Maybe a few hours away from her troubles would help her regain her perspective.

"I usually go to church on Sunday morning."

"Same here. In fact, I'd planned to leave immediately after the service. We'll have plenty of time since we won't eat lunch until one."

His hopeful expression helped make her decision. "Okay."

Jason's smile reached megawatt proportions. "Great."

"I hope I won't regret this."

"Trust me," he said. "You won't."

seven

The next morning, Jason escorted Jenna to his car after the early service. "I hope you're prepared to have a good time today. It's peaceful on the farm, and I promise we'll be home early."

"You picked a beautiful day for a drive," she said. "Are you sure your sister won't mind an extra person?"

"I'm positive. She cooks a ton of food, especially if I'm coming, and sends the leftovers with me."

"Which you thoroughly enjoy."

"Of course. I have to maintain my helpless bachelor image, you know."

Helpless was the last word Jenna would have chosen to describe the man beside her.

They gradually left the city behind. The landscape changed to an occasional house and miles and miles of golden wheat fields. Seeing the wide open spaces, the cattle grazing contentedly, and a pair of ducks swimming on a small pond, she relaxed.

"Tell me about your family," she said.

"My parents still live on a farm close to my sister Carolyn, and her husband Mark. Carolyn is two years younger than I am, and my older brother Lance lives in Kansas City. Carolyn is a music teacher. Lance and his wife Meghan, are both attorneys."

"And you have two nephews?"

"For now. Travis and Steven are six—make that seven—and nine, and every summer they spend a few days with me. Carolyn and Mark take advantage of my generosity to indulge themselves with a long weekend at a hotel, but right before school starts, they vacation as a family. Lance and Meghan are expecting their first baby in October."

He glanced at her before redirecting his attention to the highway. "What about you?"

"My family lives in Grand Island, Nebraska, along with my two brothers and sister. I don't see them as often as I'd like, but we keep in touch, especially on my nieces' birthdays."

"What brought you to this part of Kansas?"

Jenna glossed over the details. "After Chad. . .died, I finished my master's degree. Abby told me about an opening at St. Anne's, so I applied for it and here I am. Who knows, after a few years, I'll probably move on. I think I'd like Arizona."

"Why Arizona?"

Jenna shrugged. "Why not? Anyway, my sister is married to a high school principal and they have three kids, all girls."

"So Abby told you about the job at the hospital. How long have you known her?"

"We went to college together in Omaha and although we ended up at different med tech schools, we kept in touch. I was thrilled at the idea of working with her, but I didn't expect to be selected. From what I understand, there were a number of excellent applicants."

They lapsed into an easy silence for the rest of the trip. Jason turned off U.S. Highway 50 and took a few country roads before pulling onto a gravel driveway and parking on a grassy knoll behind several other vehicles.

A small group of people sat in the shade of a huge oak tree in the front yard. Instantly, she regretted her decision to come— it resembled the first time she'd met Chad's family and had to endure their scrutiny.

Two tow-headed boys ran ahead and threw themselves at Jason, latching onto his waist. "Uncle Jason, Uncle Jason, you're here. We thought you'd be late!"

"See, I've lost another tooth." Steven opened his mouth to proudly reveal a second hole in his smile.

"Good heavens!" Jason exclaimed. "The tooth fairy must be making regular stops here." He crouched down to hug Travis. "How's the birthday boy?"

"I'm just great, Uncle Jason. I'm seven now, you know."

"I know. It won't be long and I'll be coming to your wedding."

Travis made a face. "Yuck."

Carolyn stepped forward to hug her brother. "As usual, you're the last to arrive."

"Can't change my reputation," Jason teased. "Carolyn, I brought someone I'd like you to meet. Jenna Carlson."

Jenna studied Jason's sister and noted the family resemblance—especially the smile. Her tension disappeared with Carolyn's sincere welcome.

Jason scanned the crowd. "Where are Mom and Dad?"

"They're here somewhere. If you'll excuse me, I have a few last minute things to take care of before we eat."

"Can I help you?" Jenna asked.

"Thanks for offering, but I have everything under control."

"She does, too," Jason declared. "She's the control freak of the family."

Carolyn swatted his arm playfully. "I am not."

With his hand under her elbow, Jason guided Jenna along to meet his relatives and the assortment of family friends.

After lunch, birthday cake, and presents, several couples departed. Travis requested a softball game to field test his new mitt.

"Since you play ball, wouldn't you like to join us, Jenna?" Jason asked.

She sensed his underlying motive—to provide an opportunity to escape his sister's questions. "No, thanks. I'll scout out the talent instead."

"Suit yourself." He tugged a well-worn Kansas City Royals baseball cap on his head and jogged off to join the rest of his team.

Meghan wiped her forehead, then rested her hands on the mound of her stomach. "The next time I get pregnant, I'll plan it so I won't endure the summer shaped like a watermelon."

Jenna wistfully decided she wouldn't care about the season if she were fortunate enough to be expecting a baby.

"How long have you known Jason?" Carolyn asked.

Jenna forced her moment of melancholy away and answered with a cheerful tone. "Just a few weeks." She'd been expecting subtle questions regarding her relationship with the footloose male of the family now that the men weren't around. In the distance, she watched Jason help Steven assume the proper batter's stance.

"How did you meet him?"

"I was in the emergency room drawing a blood sample when my patient almost knocked me out. Jason happened to be nearby and brought the guy under control."

Esther, Jason's mother, gasped, apparently troubled at the prospect. "Were you hurt?"

"Not really. Just a granddaddy of a headache."

"We're excited Jason brought you here. It's been a long time since we've met someone he's seeing," Carolyn said.

Unable to frame a suitable comment, Jenna watched Jason perform the role of the doting uncle. *He's a natural,* she thought.

As if Carolyn had read her mind, she said, "Jason will make a wonderful father."

Jenna sensed she was fishing for a reply, but said nothing.

Carolyn continued. "He's so good with kids. I can't wait for him to have one of his own."

The offhand remark stabbed into Jenna's heart. The odds weren't favorable that she would make him—or any man, for that matter—a father. Could his family accept an adopted child? Chad's family had balked at the idea although they'd eventually accepted their son's decision.

"You say that every time Jason takes the boys," Meghan

said. "Don't make him a dad just yet. I want to take advantage of his generosity, too, before he's bogged down with his own. He won't be so anxious to take ours!"

The two other women laughed, and the tense moment for Jenna passed.

The game ended and the teams dispersed—the youngsters to play by themselves, the men to relax by their wives. Jason plopped down on the blanket in front of Jenna.

"Has Carolyn been hounding you?" he asked.

Underneath his light tone, Jenna sensed his concern. She rested her hand on his shoulder. "No, she hasn't. I've been hearing all about your childhood escapades."

Carolyn obviously understood Jenna's ploy and she answered appropriately. "You interrupted the story about locking the principal in the bathroom."

Jenna laughed, imagining a younger Jason with his lazy smile. "The principal? I don't believe it. How could you?"

"It was easy. I turned the key."

"You always were the rascal," Esther added fondly.

Jason rose, acting affronted at the audacity of his family. He reached down to pull Jenna to her feet. "We need a drink."

"But I'm not thirsty," she protested.

"Yes, you are."

Carolyn's laughter followed them to the ice chest. "Don't worry. I'll finish the story when he isn't around to interrupt."

The boys skidded to a stop near Jenna. Travis tugged on her arm. "Would you like to see Mabel and Henrietta? They're our very own heifers." His pride was unmistakable.

"I'd love to," she answered.

"Does anyone else want to come?" Steven asked.

Jason, Mark, and Lance joined her on a trek to the corral where two energetic boys showed off their four-legged pets. While Mark stayed behind to check on a sick calf, the remaining three adults proceeded to the boys' pride and joy—a tree house tucked in the sturdy limbs of an old elm tree.

Jenna marveled over their creation. As she watched the youngsters maneuver through the branches like monkeys, she wondered how Carolyn managed to keep her sanity in the face of their daring. After declining an offer to join them, she excused herself to help with supper preparations.

Once she was out of earshot, Lance clapped his hand on Jason's shoulder. "I'm impressed, brother. You've finally met a good woman."

Jason grinned.

"It's about time, too," Lance continued. "The family was beginning to question your common sense. I assume we'll be seeing more of her?"

"If I have anything to say about it, you will."

"So, she's the one."

A wry grin came to Jason's mouth. "I never could fool you, could I?"

"Not very often."

Jason stared in the direction Jenna had gone. "She's a special lady."

"Let us know when she starts picking out the china pattern. Carolyn and Meghan will be ecstatic." Lance bit his lip in apparent indecision before he continued. "Have you discussed topics like your faith and, um, a family?"

"She's a born-again Christian so we're definitely compatible in that area," Jason replied. "As for a family, she seems in favor of the idea." He read the skepticism in Lance's eyes. "Don't worry, I know Suzanne and I didn't make our feelings plain about these things early in our relationship. I won't make the same mistake."

Lance appeared relieved.

Jason couldn't resist teasing the newest father-to-be. "You realize, don't you, that my kids will be the handsomest and smartest of all the Daly grandchildren."

"Says you."

As they returned to the gathering, Jason silently offered thanks for his many blessings. God had prevented him from making a tragic mistake with Suzanne and had brought Jenna into his life.

❧

Jenna strode into the house to offer her assistance, but a trio of baby pictures on the bookcase caught her eye. Two of the infants wore boyish-type clothing and she surmised they were Carolyn's sons. However, the third child—an obvious girl from the frilly pink dress, was a mystery.

Jason hadn't mentioned having a niece. From the way the photo was centered between the boys' pictures, the child held a special place in the family.

Had Carolyn and Mark lost a baby in infancy? Jenna's heart went out to the couple. She knew precisely how they must have felt. Deep in her thoughts, the mention of her name rerouted her attention. Before she could move, she found herself eavesdropping.

"What do you think about Jenna?" Carolyn's voice was loud and clear over the rustling of potato chip bags and the clang of silverware.

"She seems very nice—just what Jason needs after all this time," Esther replied.

"Do you think he's serious about her?"

"I'd say so," Meghan interjected.

"I hope they both want the same things, otherwise he'll have the same problems he had with Suzanne. I don't want him to suffer through that again."

His disagreement over family must have been much worse than he's led me to believe, Jenna thought. *Would an adopted family make him as happy as one of his own blood?*

Gathering her wits, she entered the kitchen before she overheard any more comments. "What can I do to help?"

Carolyn pointed to two bowls. "If you'll carry the salads to the picnic table, we'll be set."

After supper, they prepared to leave. Carolyn pulled Jason aside to whisper in his ear and he replied with a broad grin. Sensing she was the topic of their furtive conversation, Jenna suddenly felt self-conscious.

Next, he approached his sister-in-law to hug her and pat her slightly rounded abdomen. "Take care of my niece or nephew."

"I will," Meghan promised.

Longing tugged at Jenna's heartstrings. *Pull yourself together,* she silently berated. *It's not supposed to hurt anymore.* She took a fortifying breath, then pasted a smile on her face.

After another chorus of good-byes and invitations for another visit, they drove away. "I like your family, Jason," Jenna said. "They're very nice people."

"I agree, but I'm prejudiced. Everyone thought you were special, too." He reached for her hand as he drove toward the highway. "But I already knew it."

Flattered by his words and attention, she smiled. After Chad's death, she'd never believed she would nor expected to experience such a thrill again. Bewildered by her recent discovery, she changed the subject. "I noticed how well the boys get along. Some kids fight all the time."

He chuckled and the charged moment passed. "They are good kids, but believe me, at times it's as if they purposely antagonize each other. Of course, I remember doing the same with Carolyn and Lance."

"My brothers are older and I know it bugged them whenever I tagged along, but they usually didn't chase me off. That's how I learned to play baseball." She smiled at the memory.

As they approached the K-96 intersection, Jason broke his handhold to steer while he flicked on his turn signal. "Did you and your husband want kids?"

"Very much so." Her voice caught in her throat, but she was pleased she sounded so normal.

"I want children, lots of them," he said. "It's crazy, but I can't wait to teach a son, or daughter, how to play ball. It will be wonderful to watch them grow and to help them learn new things."

He sounded so sure of himself—positive that his dreams would come to pass. She recognized her opening, but something held her back. "Speaking of children, I saw three baby pictures in Carolyn's living room. Who is the cute little girl? A relative?"

"Yes, and no."

His grim tone seemed out of place. "What do you mean?"

"Emily was theirs, at least for awhile. Carolyn and Mark adopted her after they had Steven. She'd had a difficult pregnancy and the doctor advised them not to try again. But Carolyn insisted she wanted a girl to round out their family."

Jenna waited with bated breath for him to continue.

"They had Emily for fourteen months before they lost her."

"I'm sorry," she murmured, thinking a condition such as Sudden Infant Death Syndrome had claimed another life. Sensing he found it difficult to talk about, she gently laid her hand on his forearm.

"Oh, she didn't die," he mentioned, as if he'd read her thoughts. "The birth mother, after twelve months, claimed she was coerced into signing relinquishment papers. An overanxious social worker from the agency, thinking she had followed all the regulations, had the teenager sign the documents twenty-four hours after Emily was born. At the time—I don't know if the rules have changed—Kansas law stipulated that a woman has to wait twelve hours after delivery before her signature is considered legal; seventy-two hours in cases of a C-section. Emily's mother had a Cesarean."

Jenna quickly grasped the error. "The mother said she was under anesthetic and therefore claimed coercion. . ."

"Exactly. The judge overturned the adoption and Emily went to live with her birth mother."

"How awful for Carolyn and Mark!" Jenna cried.

"That's an understatement."

"But they had the baby for so long."

"True. But a judge may return a child after as many as eighteen months have passed. They were four months short. Four lousy months!

"Carolyn and Mark were heartbroken. We all were. Everyone doted on that little girl, and it was like a death in the family when a case worker took her away. Carolyn was depressed for months. She finally started improving once she got pregnant with Travis. To this day, she keeps Emily's picture on display. She'd wanted a daughter so badly.

"Adoption is okay for some, but I can't suffer for eighteen months—afraid some lawyer will find a loophole. I won't put myself or my family through that again."

Jenna's spirits nose-dived. Jason sounded adamant. Would he ever change his mind?

"But that sort of thing rarely happens," she said in defense of the system. "If it did, no one would try to adopt."

"That statistic wasn't comforting to our family," he remarked dryly. "Any children I have will be my own."

Gut-wrenching sorrow pierced her heart and she bit her lip until she tasted blood. She'd wondered if an adopted family would make him happy now she knew. Her dreams had died a swift, painful death, never to be fulfilled. Their relationship was doomed before it had even had a chance. Her inability to bear the children he desired would drive a wedge between them that wouldn't be easily removed.

Jenna sat stony-faced, thankful they were only minutes from her home. With Jason's attention now on the bustling traffic, she clasped her hands together in a white-knuckled grip and held them on her lap. Out of habit, she felt for her wedding band, but the comforting presence of the gold metal was gone.

She straightened her shoulders. She'd weather this storm just as she had all the others.

At the sight of her house with its fresh primer coat, she fought the urge to run inside, slam the door, and cry her eyes out. That, however, would have to wait. Jason had to be told a few things first.

He parked the car near the curb. Before she could open her mouth to speak, he grabbed her arm. "I didn't want to overwhelm you until we spent more time together, but I want you to know something. I mean every word when I say you're important to me. . .I love you."

His sincerity shattered her fragile composure. If only he hadn't wiggled his way into her heart. . .But he had, and now, for his sake, she had to be brutally honest.

She gazed at his face, his handsome features blurred by the evening's shadows. "I never expected to feel this way again, but I love you, too. That's why we need to talk."

He frowned. "About what?"

"First, let's go inside." She slid out of his car and hurried to the front door at a near-jogging pace.

In the privacy of her home, he grasped her shoulders and pulled her to face him. "What's wrong?"

"You'd better sit down." She broke out of his hold, but he remained standing. During the few seconds' reprieve, she struggled to begin her story.

Unfortunately, the right words didn't come. Her eyes burned with unshed tears and her throat tightened. She held herself erect, feeling like a rubber band stretched to its near-breaking point.

For a long minute, she only heard his quiet breathing as he waited. Finally, he spoke.

"I can stay all night if I have to. But I'm not leaving until you tell me what this is all about."

eight

Jason watched her take a deep breath, open her mouth to speak, then close it. Her chin quivered. Whatever troubled her was apparently serious.

The vacant, expressionless look on her face tore at him. He reached out and she willingly walked into his embrace.

"It's okay, everything will work out," he murmured, stroking her hair. "Whatever it is, can't be that bad." With her head tucked under his chin, he inhaled the strawberry fragrance which he now associated exclusively with her.

After he repeated himself several times, she pushed herself away to sit stiffly on the sofa. She cleared her throat.

He joined her, poised on the edge of the couch with his knee touching hers.

"Chad and I wanted children, and we wanted them badly," she began. "To our disappointment, we couldn't have any. We went through all sorts of tests and did everything short of violating our religious principles. Finally, we went to an adoption agency. Years went by while we inched our way to the top of the waiting list. Then Chad was killed, so I withdrew our names. A month later, the agency placed a gorgeous little boy with another couple."

Jason's chest ached at her double loss.

"Considering my background and your feelings, it's best for both of us if we stop seeing each other. No matter how compatible we might be, this issue creates an irreconcilable difference between us. You want a child of your own, and I can't give you one."

She clenched her hands together. "I'm glad we discovered

this now, rather later. Don't you agree?"

Stunned by her secret, he sank against the back cushions and didn't answer. What a predicament! He'd finally found the one woman he wanted to spend the rest of his life with, but if he wanted children he'd have to subject himself to the legal system playing its own version of Russian Roulette. He couldn't lose Jenna, and yet it wouldn't be fair to her to forfeit her own dreams of family because of his fears.

A vicious circle.

"If you don't mind my asking, what exactly is the problem?"

She shrugged. "We were one of those cases where the doctors couldn't find anything wrong."

He leaned over and took her clenched hands in his. Instantly, he made a significant observation—she'd removed her wedding ring. "Maybe it will be different for us," he said, trying to be optimistic. "After all, God is still in the miracle-making business."

Her mouth trembled and her voice rose. "And what if ours never comes? How will you handle the situation then?"

"I don't know. I'll cross that bridge when I come to it."

She yanked her hands free, jammed them into her pockets, and took a deep breath. "Jason, you're in front of that bridge right now. I know the routine; the first two weeks of every month are wished away and the last two leave you stressed out with anticipation. Then you go through the crushing disappointment of knowing your miracle didn't happen and the cycle repeats itself." Her voice came out in breathless spurts. "Well, I can't, *won't,* get back on that merry-go-round again."

"You're not even willing to try—to take another chance?" he asked, incredulous.

"Speaking of taking chances, what about you? You're not willing to risk losing an adopted baby like your sister did. If it had happened to me or someone in my family, I can't say I'd be able to do it, either. But for the sake of argument, suppose adoption becomes our only alternative. Will you hate me for it? Will you distance yourself and withhold your love from that child until a magical date has passed?"

Her eyes reflected each question. She stopped, obviously waiting for a response.

He wanted to shout an emphatic denial, to tell her she was wrong, but he found himself unable to voice it. At a total loss, he ran his hands through his hair.

"I have to be honest. Right now, I can't answer you."

"I thought not," she said quietly. She rose. "It's late. You'd better go."

He ambled toward the door, his mind reeling from the blow he'd encountered. In his line of work, he'd always had a contingency plan, but he hadn't made one to cover this situation. Like Job, the things he'd feared had come to pass. His best-laid plans for his future had crumbled at his feet, leaving him empty.

Before he closed the door, he faced her. "I'll, umm, I'll call," he said, wincing at his inane comment.

She raised an eyebrow, clearly unconvinced.

"I will," he insisted.

Her face remained impassive. "Good night, Jason."

He traveled home on automatic pilot, analyzing the situation. Giving up Jenna wasn't an option; she held a part of his heart. Yet, the thought of his future family hinging on a bureaucracy terrified him. Innocent people—people like his sister and her family—paid the devastatingly high price of its mistakes.

Not only that, but with so many choices available to unwed mothers, babies were in short supply. Couples often waited years before they were fortunate enough to get one. He was thirty-four years old. He didn't have the time to wait. No, he amended, he didn't *want* to wait. And as luck would have it, he was not in a position to get his wish anytime soon.

How Jenna must have hoped that her medical problems would be an insignificant point of fact rather than an insurmountable obstacle. How she must have prayed that he'd be willing to adopt. The idea of raising children born of other parents didn't bother him; it was the possibility of losing them courtesy of legal loopholes and crafty lawyers that made him cringe.

Maybe a few days apart from each other would make everything clearer. The answer to their dilemma probably stared him in the face, but he couldn't see it.

"Heavenly Father, I know You have a solution for this situation. So I'm asking in the name of Jesus for the wisdom to make the right decision. Thank You for the answers."

❧

Jenna sank to her knees the moment Jason left, unable to restrain her pain and anguish any longer. "O God," she prayed aloud. "I'm terribly confused. I felt such a peace after I'd asked for guidance concerning Jason. Did I misread something You've tried to tell me?

"You know all things, Father God, and You knew beforehand that children are an important issue to us. And so, with this problem looming over us, I can't help but think he isn't the one You've chosen for me.

"Forgive me if I missed it, Father. And so, please take away the pain and heartache I feel. I know that You're in control of my life, and I thank you for it. I pray this in Jesus' name. Amen."

Immediately, Jenna grabbed her Bible and cuddled up in the recliner. It fell open, and Proverbs 3:5, "Trust in the Lord with all thine heart; and lean not unto thine own understanding," leapt off the page.

She remembered a verse about God's thoughts and ways being above mortal men's, but making observations and weighing facts in order to arrive at logical conclusions was a deeply ingrained practice. Was the Lord telling her something? Was this one time she shouldn't be so quick to do what came naturally?

Still searching for answers, she turned to the Psalms. Ignoring the time, she read well into the night and stopped only when the telephone rang.

She picked up the receiver, but her greeting wasn't returned. "Who's calling?" she demanded.

Again, silence replied.

"Whom do you want to talk to?" she asked.

"You're the one, Jenna Carlson," a voice rasped.

She froze. The sinister tone sent a shiver running down her spine. Determined not to give him the weapon of fear, she demanded, "I'm listening. What do you want?"

An eerie laugh sounded in her ear.

"What do you want? Who is this?"

A dial tone answered, and she replaced the receiver. Wary from the incident, she rechecked her deadbolt locks. Maybe having a dog around wasn't such a bad idea.

A few minutes later, the phone jangled again and she jumped. Slowly, deliberately, she picked up the handset.

"Hello?"

This time, the heavy silence made her fear mushroom to gigantic proportions. Immediately, she broke the connection.

It rang again and this time, she waited for the answering machine to take over.

"I know you're there," the voice singsonged. She rushed into her bedroom to avoid hearing the rest of his ramblings. At least she'd have a taped conversation to hand over to the police.

Suddenly the events of the past week, coupled with tonight's calls, no longer seemed like pranks. Something diabolical was at work.

She reached for a phone book in the nightstand drawer, then stopped herself. Jason wasn't part of her life any longer. She couldn't call him. Like every other problem she'd encountered since Chad's death, this problem was one she would handle alone.

~

The next morning, Abby sat on the edge of her friend's desk to chat. "Am I interrupting? You know you shouldn't have such a dismal expression—it causes wrinkles. Problems today?"

"No more than usual for a Monday, I guess," Jenna replied. "By the way, have you gotten any weird phone calls lately?"

"No, but since you're asking, I assume you have."

"Yeah. He either doesn't say a word, or he says he's calling for me. He has this funny little laugh, too."

Abby's eyes were wide and reflected her concern. "Good heavens, Jen! First the trash, then the battery and your house, and now this. Have you reported it?"

Jenna tapped a pencil on the desk. "Yeah. The police suggested I get a caller ID unit to track down the person responsible. They also recommended an unlisted phone number. Unfortunately, if I get one while John is gone, I'll defeat my purpose. I'd have to give it out to everyone in case someone needed me."

She sighed. "Although the second option is the one I prefer, I'm going to buy a phone ID system. Between that and my answering machine, I'm screening all calls."

"Have you told Jason?" Abby looked around, trying to catch a glimpse of the security consultant. "I thought he was working here for a few more days."

"I haven't seen him or his assistant, Burrows, either." Jenna expected Jason to appear at any moment and the tension was making her head ache.

Abby reached for the phone. "I'll call Bruce."

Jenna forestalled her. "He has enough to worry about. Please, don't bother him."

"Then tell Jason. He'll know what to do."

Jenna realigned a stack of papers. "I'm already following the police's advice."

Abby grabbed her hand. "No ring, I see," she said, with a knowing nod. "Does this mean what I think—?"

Jenna pulled free. Her "No," was emphatic. "We're not seeing each other any more."

Abby's jaw dropped. "Why not? I thought everything was fine."

"It wasn't. Our plans concerning a family don't mesh. Therefore, it's over."

"He doesn't want children?"

"It's a long story," Jenna began.

"I have time." Abby crossed her legs as if planning to wait. Jenna capitulated and recited a condensed version of the story leading to their stalemate.

"Oh, Jen. I'm so sorry."

"Hey, don't be. I'm thankful for discovering the problem now, rather than later." She felt Abby's scrutiny. "Don't worry. I'm okay; I can handle it."

At odd moments throughout the day, disappointment and sorrow threatened to overtake her and she quoted Proverbs 3:5 to hold those emotions at bay. However, when Burrows arrived to finish the employee review Jason had started, her hopes for a friendly parting died. Rejection and bitterness wanted to take root, and she struggled to find forgiveness in her heart.

Work occupied her thoughts, but at home, it became exceedingly hard to find the inner peace she craved. To combat her doldrums, she plugged in a praise tape and turned the volume up high while she baked double-chocolate fudge brownies. Then she knitted furiously, accomplishing more in an hour than ever before. But when she caught herself listening for the telephone, she escaped outside.

Knowing she wouldn't sleep unless she was exhausted, she bicycled through the park until the sun's rays faded into twilight. By the time she pedaled home, she was proud of her accomplishments—she was tired and she had survived her first twenty-four hours without Jason.

❧

John Masters returned to work on Thursday and Jenna gave him a thorough briefing. Part of her was sorry not to have the additional duties which had kept her mind off of her personal problems. On the other hand, she was relieved to have her unlisted telephone number placed into service.

She'd hoped the caller ID unit would reveal the identity of the instigator, but it hadn't. For each call he'd made, the display had read "Not available." At least the answering machine saved her from dealing directly with him, but she didn't know if the taped version was easier to handle than the real thing. Hearing either one gave her the willies.

"I know you're there," he had rasped during his last message. "Pleasant dreams."

As she was sure he had intended, pleasant dreams quickly fled. Even now, remembering his voice sent shivers crawling down her spine. Tomorrow afternoon, she planned to turn the tape over to the police. Maybe they would find a connection between her vandals and the anonymous caller.

That evening at the ball game, before she had the opportunity to say hello, Abby pulled her away from listening ears. "Have you heard the news about Jason?"

Jenna's heart skipped a beat. "No. What?"

"He went to Oklahoma City this week. While he was there, an irate husband of one of his clients broadsided him. Totaled his vehicle."

"Oh dear. Was he. . . ?" She couldn't finish the thought. A vision of Jason lying in a casket brought forth a vivid memory of gladioli and the cloying scent of roses. Her stomach churned. She hated roses.

"He's fine. Banged up a little. He'll be back on Monday."

Jenna's relief traveled down to her baseball cleats. *Thank you, God.*

"You look pale. He's fine, really." Abby's tone was reassuring. Suddenly, her eyes narrowed. "You still care for him, don't you?"

Jenna avoided her friend's gaze. "I don't want to see anyone hurt, that's all." She drew a slip of paper out of her side pocket. "Here's my new unlisted phone number. Please don't give it to anyone."

"What about Jason?"

"What about him?"

"What if he wants to talk to you?" Abby persisted.

"He knows where to find me."

❧

Early Friday evening, Jason stood on his sister's doorstep and knocked.

"Jason! What brings you here?" Carolyn exclaimed, ushering him inside.

"Hi, sis. It's good to see you, too. Easy on the ribs, though."

"What's wrong?"

"An accidental, on-purpose car wreck." He grinned at his contradictory description. "A man I tracked down last year for back child support decided to play a little rough."

Carolyn was aghast. "In Wichita?"

He shook his head. "Oklahoma City. Regardless, I was on my way home and decided to stop by."

"Correct my geography, but Hutchinson comes *after* Wichita, not before. A hundred-and-some mile detour isn't exactly a spur-of-the-moment visit. What's on your mind?"

"I have a problem and I need your opinion."

"Ah," she said, sounding smug as she poured two tall glasses of soda. "Woman trouble."

"Yeah. Jenna can't have kids and wants to adopt. After seeing what you went through with Emily, I've always said I'd never put myself in a similar situation. Now I'm facing a double-edged sword," he finished ruefully.

"Sounds like it."

"I need some advice, Linnie," he said, using her childhood nickname.

She placed the glass in front of him, then sat across the kitchen table. "I've learned one thing in my relatively short life—you can never say 'never.' The way I see it, you have three choices. One, you can either eat your words, grit your teeth, and pray your experience with adoption won't be similar to mine; two, totally break off your relationship with Jenna and hope for better luck next time; or three, stay with Jenna and resign yourself to never having a family of any kind. The last option, however, depends upon Jenna. She may decide to wait for someone who doesn't have the same fears you do."

He stroked the moisture off the sides of his tumbler. "That's what I came up with too," he said wearily. "Breaking up with Jenna isn't an attractive option, because I do love her. I can't shut off my feelings like a faucet." He leaned forward. "Tell me, sis, would you have tried to adopt again if Travis hadn't come along?"

Carolyn looked thoughtful. "That's a tough question. Losing Emily was almost like she had died. And she did—to us anyway. It was a dark period for all of us.

"Every day I consoled myself with one thought—Emily's mother loves her and is caring for her. You also can't imagine how often I've quoted Romans 8:28. I don't know what good thing God has planned to come out of the bad situation, and I may never know, but He's in charge of my life. Emily's, too. So, I'll always pray for her and her mother."

She clutched his hand. "You can't allow my experience to influence your decision. If Jenna is the woman God has chosen for you, then don't let fear rob you of something wonderful. To finally answer your question, I think we'd have tried again. Eventually."

"Speaking of fear, Jenna's always been afraid of my job. Her husband was killed in the line of duty and she's leery of men in law-enforcement or related careers. Even if we work out the adoption issue, she'll step on the brakes once she learns about my accident."

"Then you both need to study 1 John 4:18," Carolyn declared. "It's about love casting out fear."

With the verse committed to memory, Jason pushed the speed limit on his way home. Although his watch showed it was nearly ten P.M., the urge to talk to Jenna gnawed at him. He grabbed his cellular phone and punched her number from memory.

A sharp note clanged in his ear before a recording informed him the number was no longer in service. Thinking he'd misdialed, he tried again and obtained the same message. Mystified, he called directory assistance.

"I don't have a listing for a Jenna Carlson," the operator reported.

"What about J. Carlson?"

"I'm sorry."

"Has her phone been disconnected or did she request an unlisted—"

"I really can't say, sir."

He knew the woman followed proper protocol, but it didn't hurt to try. After thanking the operator, he dialed another number.

"Abby, this is Jason. I tried phoning Jenna, but her phone's been disconnected. What's going on?"

She didn't answer.

"Abby, did you hear me?"

"I heard you. You may as well know; she requested an unlisted number."

"Do you have it?"

"Yes, I do," she said warily, "but she instructed me not to give it to anyone."

"I see." He bit his lip, guessing the reason for her cool tone. "If you won't tell me her number, at least tell me why she changed it." He knew where she lived and worked. Changing her phone number would be a drastic, but futile move to ensure he'd leave her alone.

"She's been getting some weird phone calls. Even though she shrugs them off as unimportant, I think she's scared."

Abby's observation made his concern grow. Jenna wasn't the type of person to frighten easily. "Has she had any more trouble at home?"

"You're really worried, aren't you?"

"Don't sound so surprised. Of course, I am," he snapped.

There were a few seconds of silence. "Jason?" her voice warmed a few degrees.

He waited.

"I told her about your accident. For what it's worth, she was worried about you, too."

"So will you give me the number?"

"I want to, but I can't. I promised."

"Then I'll drive to her house." He didn't care how late it was, he wanted to talk to her.

"It won't do any good. She isn't there."

"Where is she?"

"She went to Nebraska for the weekend."

A few more days won't matter, he told himself. But first thing Monday morning, he'd find her. Seven days without her were seven days too many.

nine

Late Monday morning, Jenna strode into the lab's lounge. Her weekly meeting with the IV therapy nurses had gone well and now she was anxious to raid the snack machine.

As she dialed her locker combination, she noticed one of the adjoining lockers was open. After selecting the exact change from her purse and securing her belongings again, she reached across to shut the door.

It wouldn't close.

Thinking something was caught in the hinge, she intended to fix the problem. A flash of gold made her hand freeze in mid-air.

There in the semi-darkness, lay an expensive watch in the otherwise empty locker.

Why, would anyone—? Her puzzlement turned into suspicion. She latched the door, then scanned the staff bulletin board for "Lost and Found" notices. Nothing had been reported, so she cornered her boss in his office.

"John, I think I've found a stolen wristwatch in our lounge."

"Maybe it belongs to one of our employees."

She shook her head. "I've already checked the board. I doubt anyone would leave such an expensive item in an unsecured locker."

"Call Security."

She hesitated. "Maybe *you* should. You're the boss." Her excuse sounded feeble, but she wasn't ready to talk to Jason Daly, yet.

"Nonsense. If they have any questions, you're the one to answer them."

Knowing her superior was right, she reluctantly dialed the extension and asked for Bruce. "I've found a watch," she said after a brief greeting. "Has anyone reported one missing?"

"What's the description?"

She gave it. Immediately, she overheard him confer with someone in the background. Before she could respond, the owner of a familiar baritone replaced Bruce.

"Where did you find it?" he asked.

Her heart leaped at the sound of Jason's voice, but she compelled herself to speak calmly. "In our lounge."

His admonition of, "Don't touch anything. We'll be right there," confirmed her hunch and fear shot down her spine.

Would this latest episode put her back on the list of suspects?

She returned to the break room seconds before the two men appeared in the doorway.

"Good grief, guys. Did you run? It's only been five minutes since I called." She'd hoped for more time to mentally prepare herself for Jason's unavoidable appearance, but her wish hadn't been granted. He stood before her, as tall and handsome as ever, and apparently none the worse for his accident.

"I was on my way here when you called," Jason replied.

She blinked, taken aback by his comment. Unnerved by his tender expression, she broke eye contact and simply pointed to locker eighteen. "I found it open and only touched the handle."

Using a pencil, Jason scooted the jewelry forward and pushed it into a transparent sandwich bag.

She wanted her suspicions confirmed. "It's stolen, isn't it?"

Jason was solemn-faced. "If it isn't, it's a remarkable duplicate."

"Who's assigned to this locker?" Bruce asked.

"Probably no one. We advise all employees to secure their possessions in order to deter sticky fingers, and since this one was empty. . ." She shrugged.

Jason inspected the watch through the clear plastic. "Can you check your records to make certain?"

Jenna left and returned five minutes later, hating the report she had to relay. "According to my information, this is Sam's—Samuel Todd's—locker."

Bruce and Jason looked at each other. "We'd like to talk to him."

It couldn't be Sam, it just couldn't! It was inconceivable to even think one of her friends was a possible criminal. "Sam wouldn't steal anything!" she insisted.

"Is he here? We'd like to ask a few questions," Jason said patiently, but firmly.

With a heavy heart, she directed them to the conference room. "I'll get him," she said.

A few minutes later, the four of them were assembled.

"Sam, our records show you are assigned to locker eighteen. Is that correct?" Jenna asked.

Sam nodded his head, clearly puzzled. "Yes, but I haven't used it for about a week. Why?"

"I found a watch in it that Mr. Edwards and Mr. Daly suspect is stolen property."

Sam's face mirrored his shock. "And you think I had something to do with it?"

"No. . .we just had to. . ."

Jason interrupted. "Why aren't you using the locker?"

"My padlock jammed and I broke it when I jimmied it open. I rarely use the locker during the summer months, so I haven't bought a replacement, yet."

Interrogated for an additional fifteen minutes, a visibly shaken Sam returned to his work station while Bruce left for his office.

"What happens now?" Jenna demanded, ready to defend Sam with her last breath.

Jason shrugged. "Nothing. We wait and see."

Jen relaxed. "Then you don't think Sam did it!"

"I won't agree or disagree, but he doesn't have a strong alibi at the time the watch was stolen. If we're lucky, we'll pick up some useful fingerprints."

Jenna set her jaw. "It isn't Sam."

He laid one hand on her shoulder. "I know how you feel, but let me do my job. Okay?"

His touch was bittersweet. "Okay. By the way, Abby mentioned your accident. How are you?" She spoke in a nonchalant manner to hide her concern.

"Bruised ribs. Nothing major."

"I'm glad."

"I heard you went out of town, too."

She stared at a point over his shoulder. "I needed a break."

Realizing his hand hadn't moved, she tried to step back. Before she could wiggle away, he tightened his grip.

"Can you spare about five minutes to talk?" he asked.

She narrowed her eyes. "About what?"

"Us."

She shook her head. "Sorry, Jason. There is no 'us,' unless you have a toad in your pocket."

He released her to run one hand through his hair. "I know I reacted badly the other evening and I apologize. I wish I could say that I've changed my opinions this past week, but I can't. I am asking though, for time to try."

Touched by his heartfelt speech, tears welled in her eyes and she chewed on her bottom lip.

"After hearing about my little accident, your fears about my job have skyrocketed, right?" At her slow nod, he added, "So while I'm developing an open mind, I'd like you to do the same." He paused. "But even if you tell me right now that you don't love me, I still want to help you."

"That's the problem," she murmured. "I do love you."

He grabbed both of her hands. "Carolyn gave me a Scripture

verse about love casting out fear. Shall we test God at his Word?"

Her gaze locked on Jason's. His whole expression pleaded for mercy. The proverbial fork in the road faced her, and now the question of "Would she go it alone?" had to be answered. It was a hard decision, yet it wasn't.

Slowly she nodded.

He immediately enfolded her in his warm embrace. His woodsy scent made her feel as if she'd finally come home. Caught up in a maelstrom of emotions ranging from utter happiness to sheer relief, tears slipped down her cheeks.

"I'm getting you all wet," she hiccuped.

He cupped her face and brushed away the glistening trail. "I couldn't care less. In any event, I'm coming by this evening to discuss your phone calls."

"There's no need, Jason. I've already talked to the police and taken my tape to the station. I've also changed my phone number, so I'm sure I won't be bothered any more."

"Don't argue." His smile softened the order and he released her rather reluctantly. "Six o'clock. Be there."

With a spring in her step, she returned to her desk. The day had brightened and she could hardly wait until the end of her shift.

To her dismay, her happiness faded mid-afternoon.

The phone on her desk rang and she answered by rote. No one returned her greeting and she attributed it to a faulty receiver. She'd been begging for a new phone for weeks because of the static on the line, maybe now she'd receive a replacement.

As she lowered the receiver, an eerie laugh made her freeze. A heartbeat later, she slammed down the receiver.

Fear swept over her in icy sheets. She'd always felt anonymous among the hundreds of St. Anne's employees. How had he learned her extension number? Realistically, it wouldn't be too difficult for a determined person to discover her whereabouts. Or was it someone she knew?

Without wasting time, she dialed Jason's office. To her consternation, neither he nor Bruce were available. Her only alternative was to leave a message.

And pray.

≈

At home, Jenna couldn't believe time could pass so slowly. Anxious for six o'clock to roll around, she knitted several more inches on her afghan. At this rate, she'd complete her project much sooner than she'd ever anticipated.

She fought the urge to watch for Jason's arrival, hoping his habit for punctuality hadn't changed. To her great joy, the doorbell rang as her watch beeped the hour. Excited, she dropped her needles and yarn in a heap and flung open the front door.

"Do you do that all the time?" Jason's voice held a sharp edge.

"Do what? Let people in who ring the bell? Of course I do," she answered pertly. "That's the idea, isn't it?"

He stepped across the threshold carrying two brown paper bags. "Don't you ever check to see who it is first? Any jerk could be outside, waiting to pounce on you."

She closed the door. "Pardon me for not checking the peephole, but since it is six o'clock—the time you told me you'd be here—I didn't feel it was necessary to look," she retorted. "If you don't mind, I'd rather not argue over my door-opening habits."

Glancing at him, she noticed a few changes—a crisp new haircut and small nicks on his face. "Looks like you took one step too close to your razor," she teased. "You need to be more careful."

He flashed his lopsided grin. "I'm afraid so."

"So what's in the bags?"

"Motion detector lights and window locks. I'm assuming

your phone caller is also the one responsible for the vandalism. If so, I don't want to make things easy for him in case he decides he wants inside."

The blood drained from her face. She hadn't considered the possibility.

"There's no reason to think he's interested," Jason soothed, as if he realized he'd given her a new worry. "I'm just overly cautious."

He placed the bags on the kitchen table. "By the way, I called Abby after I couldn't reach you last night. She refused to give me your new phone number."

She smiled. "I knew she wouldn't."

"Were you ever going to give it to me?"

"Not unless you asked for it, and I didn't think you would."

His gaze grew intent. "You were wrong."

Jenna recited the number, noticing that he committed it to memory.

He sat down in one of her oak dining chairs. "I want to hear more about your phone incidents."

She shrugged. "There isn't a lot to tell. He's called several times, and I usually listen to him breathe. He also has the spookiest laugh. I can't tell if it's normal for him or if he's simply disguising it."

"What does he say?"

"He usually says he's calling for me. After I started letting my answering machine pickup, he would say that he knew I was here. Since he was always right, I assume he was nearby, but I never saw a strange car in the vicinity."

"Could it be a neighbor?"

"No. Frieda Burns lives next door and she doesn't get out much. The Hills just came back from vacation and they're busy with their two teenagers, Amy and Andrew. The Marvins left several days ago to visit their grandchildren in Oklahoma."

Jason jotted down a few notes in his notepad. "What about

the house with the 'For Sale' sign?"

"It's been vacant for about two months. The Millers moved to Goodland and, as far as I know, only the realtor has a key."

Jason looked thoughtful. "And you're sure it's a man."

"Yes."

"How does he sound?"

"What do you mean?"

"His breathing, how does it sound? Long deep breaths, short fast ones, what?" he asked patiently.

Jenna bit her lip and wrinkled her forehead as she tried to remember. "I don't know, long deep breaths, I guess. Possibly forced. I haven't tried to evaluate them."

"Does he call at a certain time?"

"It varies. Today was unusual because he contacted me at work."

"At work?" he echoed, clearly shocked. "Why didn't you say something?"

"I telephoned you, but you weren't in your office. I left a message for you with the secretary."

"Bruce and I were checking some of the floors. Next time, page me," he ordered. "In the meantime, I'll have a chat with Monica."

She placed a hand over his. "Please don't be upset with her. She asked if it was urgent and I told her no, since I'd see you this evening. No harm done."

"Don't do it again," he said, his voice grim. "The next time he bothers you, I want to know immediately. I'll talk to Bruce—see what precautions we can take."

"Precautions? What makes you think—"

"He can't harass you at home, so he apparently intends to catch you at the hospital. Can you arrange for someone to screen your calls?"

"Get serious, Jason."

"I don't suppose you can change your extension number."

She shook her head and he pressed on, "so I want you to log the time of day, what you're doing, where you're at, and how long he stays on the phone. If he says anything, anything at all, write it down. Got it?"

"Got it."

"And don't go anywhere by yourself."

She shook her head. "Not possible. In case you've forgotten, I live alone. As for the hospital, I can't pull someone from their duties to follow me around."

His eyes narrowed. "It might be someone you know."

"I've thought of that," she said. "Although I can't imagine who. My coworkers seem so trustworthy."

"Someone isn't," Jason reminded her. "Until we find him or her, keep your doors locked. And whatever you do, *use the peephole* before you let anyone in!"

As much as she hated the restriction, she had no choice. "You're the expert," she said, using a resigned tone.

His eyes took on a gleam of satisfaction. "Since we've settled that, what do you say we order a pizza while I put my handyman skills to use? Thin crust, with all the toppings and extra black olives?"

She grinned. "I thought you'd never ask."

≈

The next morning, promptly at eight, Jason and Bruce walked into the lab. Although the preliminary investigation hadn't unearthed any real suspects, they both agreed on one important issue: finding two stolen articles in the lab seemed too coincidental.

After a brief conversation with John Masters, the trio approached Jenna. John interrupted her conversation with a maintenance man.

"Jenna," John said. "These gentlemen want to review some of our records. I'm on my way to a quality assurance meeting, so would you have time to work with them?"

"No problem."

"Wonderful. Gentlemen, I'll leave you in Jenna's hands."

John strode toward the nearest exit while she turned back to the young man in the khaki-colored uniform. "After these cabinets are moved into storage, Harry, the microbiology people need your help. If you have any problems, I'll be around."

"Okay." Harry, a young man in his mid-twenties, sauntered away.

She glanced at Jason. "How can I help you?"

"We want to cross-check our victims against the lab staffing schedule to see if we can find a pattern," Jason said. "Is that possible?"

"Sure. The information is stored on computer. Since you don't have clearance to access our information system, you can log on with my code."

"Perfect." Jason glanced around the lab. "I don't mean to complain, but can we work someplace more private?"

She thought a moment. "Use John's office. He has meetings scheduled all morning so I don't expect him back until after lunch."

Once there, Jenna typed in her lab ID and her personal password while Jason pulled his notebook from his shirt pocket and flipped to a page covered in his large handwriting. He read off the names and dates.

"You're in luck," she said, typing in a three-letter mnemonic to access the specimen receiving module. "Those patient encounters should still be in the computer. Its memory only stores three months of activity in the current files. Then, we archive the data. At that point, it's a much more involved process to retrieve any information, although it can be done."

She paused, waiting for the screen she wanted to appear. "Here we go. At this prompt," she pointed to the cursor, "Press HELP. Then type in the patient's name and select the date in question. Like this." She demonstrated with the first name on his list. "Press HELP again, and you'll see the time the sample was drawn and the time it was received in our department. When you're finished, press the ESCAPE key, and start over. Any questions?"

"No," Jason said, his attention fixed on the monitor.

She rose. "If you run into a problem, I'll be right outside. Want a cup of coffee?"

"Not right now." He grinned. "Ask me again, later."

Bruce and Jason pored over the computer's data. It didn't take long for Jason to pinpoint an interesting piece of evidence. After making a mental note, he proceeded to the next case. To his surprise, the same detail applied to the second victim, then a third. He held his counsel until he reviewed the remaining patient records.

By the time he finished, an ache had settled between his shoulder blades. He leaned back, rubbed his neck, and pondered his findings. In all but one case involving patients, a specific person had been in the room sometime prior to the individuals noticing their losses.

Jason studied Bruce and waited for the other man to react. Surely he, too, had found the common denominator.

Bruce whistled. "I'd never have believed it if I hadn't seen it for myself. The idea is too bizarre to be believable."

"I know."

Bruce squared his jaw and met Jason's gaze. "What do you think is going on?"

Jason pressed his mouth into a hard line. "First of all, Jenna is innocent. I know it in my gut."

Bruce appeared relieved.

"That leaves only one explanation."

"Which is?"

Jason stared at her initials on the screen. "Someone is framing Jenna, and doing a good job of it, too."

ten

"Who could it be?" Bruce asked, incredulous.

Jason rubbed his chin. "I don't know, but whoever it is, he's out to get her." He tapped his pencil on the table. "Now that I think about it, her problems at home probably tie in with those here. He's using an old military strategy—attack on two fronts."

"But why Jenna? She's basically new in town and gets along with everybody."

"Again, I don't know." What was the motive behind her harassment? Did the man pick her out of a hat, or did he have a personal vendetta?

"Making harassing phone calls is one thing, but framing her for a crime doesn't make sense."

"I agree, but this person has obviously spent a great deal of time planning his moves. This isn't a spur of the moment thing on his part. It's definitely premeditated."

Bruce's expression became troubled. "What do we do now and what will you tell Payce? He's itching to throw the book at the culprit. If we tell him about Jenna. . ."

"I'll handle it. Now that we know what we're up against, we can plan accordingly. In the meantime, it's business as usual. If our fellow thinks he's getting away scot-free, he'll become careless and make a mistake. We're due for a break."

A few days later, the break Jason had been waiting for appeared. He found Jenna peering into a small analyzer. Her lips moved soundlessly and her brow was furrowed in concentration as she replaced some sort of valve and syringe mechanism.

"Hi, there," he whispered in her ear.

Startled, she jumped and turned. "Jason! You scared me to death! Don't you know it's not polite to sneak up on someone!" Her smile softened the harsh scolding.

"Miss me?" He grinned a little-boy grin.

"You should know better than to ask. Of course I do."

"May I steal you away for a few minutes?"

"Let me put this together first." She closed the front panel and pressed a button. Lights flashed and the words "calibration in progress" appeared. Satisfied, she walked toward the sink.

"Bad day?" she asked, washing her hands.

"I've had better. . .and worse. A patient reported money missing from her purse this morning and we're wading through everyone's testimony."

"So the thief's at it again. Who was the victim, or is that privileged information?"

"A Ms. Remington."

"Fourth floor?" Jenna's face paled at Jason's nod. "I was in her room this morning."

"I know."

"You know?" Her face turned chalky white. "You think I stole the money, don't you?"

"We need to talk." He guided her to the relative privacy of the lab's lounge and closed the door.

"Admit it," Jenna demanded. "You still suspect me, don't you?"

Jason rubbed his neck. "I can't believe you still don't trust me."

His wounded expression cut through her like a knife. She laid a hand on his arm. "I'm sorry. I should, but when even *I* can see my connection to these events. . ." her voice faded.

He smiled, appearing to accept her explanation. "Someone is trying to frame you and I think it's your anonymous caller."

"But why?" Her eyes were wide and troubled.

"I don't know. Have you had an argument with anyone, made any enemies?"

"No. Absolutely not."

"Don't go anywhere alone. Be sure someone you trust is with you or at least within arm's reach. Whoever has orchestrated this knows your habits very well."

"Maybe I should take some vacation time."

"No!" He lowered his voice. "If the crook is trying to pin the crimes on you, he'll stop while you're gone. We need to draw him out and that means you have to be on duty. I wonder. . ." He stopped in mid-thought. "I'll be back as soon as I can. If the guy calls, try to make him talk. We need to find out why he's targeted you."

Jason kissed her quickly, then strode from the room.

"Make him talk," she mimicked. "I don't like this cops-and-robbers game one bit!"

She returned to her desk and tried to hide her agitation each time the phone rang. After several false alarms, she relaxed her guard.

Thirty minutes later, preoccupied with the report in her hand, she answered the phone without thinking.

"Well, well, how are you today?" a raspy voice inquired. "I called in a tip about there being stolen money in your desk. I can't wait to see you carted off to jail."

His chuckle sent chills through her. "Who are you? Why are you doing this?" She sounded frantic, but she didn't care. If he wanted to scare her, he had succeeded.

"You have something that isn't yours, and you're going to pay for it. When you're gone, it will go to the rightful person."

"What do I have that isn't mine?"

The click reverberated in her ear before the dial tone sounded.

Her heart pounded. *Remember what he said. Write it down.* Money, he'd said money was in her desk. She whipped through the papers on her desk. Nothing.

In *the desk, not* on *it*, she reminded herself.

Working her way down, she rifled through the contents of each drawer until she reached the bottom one. Afraid of what she'd find, she took a deep breath before she yanked it open.

A corner of green caught her eye and her stomach churned. Wary, she scooted the manila envelope aside with the eraser-end of a pencil and stared. A twenty and three tens.

With damp palms and deliberate movements, she closed the drawer, lifted the receiver and punched a number from memory.

❧

"Let's go over this again," Jason said, his gaze following Jenna's movements as she paced her kitchen floor.

"I don't want to go over this again," she said impatiently. "I'm tired and I'm nervous. I need to do something besides play twenty questions, like bake a cake or something!" If ever she'd experienced a time when beating, chopping, and blending would help, this was it. Under the circumstances, knitting was simply too tame an activity.

"Go ahead."

She assembled her ingredients, aware he was biding his time. Finally, she gave in and brought the subject up herself. "I can't add anything to what I said a few hours ago."

"You never know what you may remember. Just tell me what happened."

She sprinkled spices into her homemade spaghetti sauce, then cracked two eggs into a bowl of chocolate cake batter. "He said he'd reported the money in my desk and told me I had something that didn't belong to me—something that would go to the rightful person. Then, he cut me off before I could ask any more questions."

"You have something that doesn't belong to you." Jason recited the caller's words thoughtfully. "What do you have that isn't yours?"

"I haven't the slightest idea. I haven't bought anything of value in years."

Jason looked around the room. "What about this house? Did you have any trouble leasing this place? Did you outbid someone to get it?"

"Not that I know of." Her head throbbed from the stress and his relentless questions. "Do you mind if we drop this for now?" She tasted the sauce. Satisfied with the seasoning, she turned the burner's setting to simmer before sliding the cake pan into the oven.

"Okay, we'll take a break. Something may come to mind later." He leaned over the skillet. "Hey, this smells delicious."

"It should. I begged the recipe from a friend of mine who's a full-blooded Italian. Want some?"

Jason smiled. "I thought you'd never ask."

"The sauce won't be ready for awhile. Why don't you read the paper or catch the evening news?"

He tugged her into his arms. "I'm sorry I wasn't with you when the call came."

"Hey, don't worry, I handled it."

He clutched her tighter. "Promise me you'll be careful, wherever you go. Whether it's at home or at work."

"I promise. Now, if you don't mind, please read the paper and leave the cook alone," she scolded playfully.

After she set the table, she joined him on the sofa, leaned back, and enjoyed the silence. A quiet house provided a welcomed respite from the noisy, fast pace of her job.

She closed her eyes, hearing crinkling noises as he turned the pages. The unremarkable noise, along with the aroma wafting out of the kitchen, soon brought fantasies of marriage. How wonderful to be a couple passing the early evening hours in companionable silence. Although she'd loved Chad, he was gone. She'd spent years thinking she'd be alone but lately, she'd come to a new realization.

She wanted to experience this scene every night with Jason beside her.

Please Lord, I'm anxious for our love to cast out all of our fears. Help me to be patient and give him the time he needs.

She picked up the local life section of the newspaper out of the pile on the coffee table, glanced at a few photos, then flipped to an advice column.

A headline jumped off one page. *Parents Lose Battle over Child Custody.*

Jenna skimmed the article, grasping only a few choice words and phrases. Dismayed at its timeliness and subsequent effect on her own life, she reread the piece, this time digesting the information.

> In a case involving a prominent local family, Judge Tomlinson has ruled that the adoption of Mark and Mary Swenson's twelve-month old son, Alan, is invalid. According to sources, the birth father has contested the adoption, citing failure of the birth mother to notify him of her legal intentions. A 1979 Kansas statute requires that the birth father, when known, must be informed and give his consent. Attorneys for the mother claim that every effort was made to locate the man and all attempts were unsuccessful. The Swensons were unable to be reached for comment.

Her eyes filled with tears. If Jason saw this story, his opinion concerning adoption would be etched in stone—absolutely nothing would convince him to change his mind. With her hands shaking, she meticulously refolded the paper.

"Did you read this section?" she asked.

"Not yet."

Jenna handed the newsprint to him. "There are a few fascinating pieces, especially the one on page ten." She turned to the real estate ads and waited while he glanced at the article.

He stiffened.

She hardly breathed, anxious for his comment.

He turned the page and continued reading.

She wanted him to say something, anything. "Did you see the story?"

"Yes."

"And?"

He lifted his shoulders, appearing nonchalant about the subject. "What do you want me to say? The Swensons have my sympathy because I know what they're going through right now. I wouldn't be surprised if this happens more often than not. Their case is newsworthy because they're prominent business people. How many others never make the headlines?"

"I don't believe there are that many," she said firmly. "The people who work with adoptive and birth parents try hard to give a baby a good home."

"I'm sure they do, but they make mistakes; they're only human. I wonder, though, when someone will do a study on these kids and discover the psychological harm caused by their legal mistakes."

Although Jenna agreed those were extremely difficult times for all parties involved, she also felt the benefits of adoption were worth the risk. If only Jason would quit hanging onto his qualms like a dog with a bone. Immediately, she reminded herself of Proverbs 3:5 and I John 4:18.

Lord, I thank you for being in control and for working in Jason's heart. Help me not to be so impatient when he doesn't see things the same way I do.

"On the other hand," Jason mentioned, "My neighbor, Tom Farley, asked if I'd be a reference for them on their adoption application. He and his wife want to add an older boy to their family."

"That's wonderful," she exclaimed.

He shrugged. "Who knows? I hope they understand the risks they're taking." He folded the paper haphazardly and tossed it onto the classifieds. "I'm starved. Do you think dinner is ready yet?"

As if on cue, the oven timer buzzed. "I'd say so," she said, hiding her disappointment behind a smile. "Let's eat."

"What shall we do this evening?" he asked, spooning sauce over the spaghetti on her plate.

"I don't know. How about a movie? It's too hot to be outdoors."

"A movie it is." He tasted his entree. "This is good. My compliments to the cook."

"Thank you." She swallowed a few bites before the telephone rang. Tossing her napkin next to her plate, she crossed the kitchen to answer.

Almost immediately, her stomach churned. "Where are you?" she asked, stretching the phone cord around the doorway to peer outside the living room window.

Jason moved to her side. "What's wrong?" he mouthed, his eyebrows drawn into a single line.

She replaced the receiver and sank into the nearest chair.

"Who was it?" he demanded.

"It was him. The same guy who's been calling."

"You're kidding."

"I wish I was."

"How in the world did he get your number?"

She shrugged.

"What did he say?" He scraped another chair across the floor and lifted her hands into his lap. "What did he say?" he repeated, his baritone steel-edged.

"He said he's under our noses. You can't find him and there's nothing you can do about it." She met his gaze. "He knows you're here."

Jason ran his fingers through his hair. Seconds later, he

jumped to his feet, transformed into a well-trained, objective investigator. He punched numbers from memory, issued orders to his staff. He even called Bruce.

While Jason busied himself with details, Jenna scraped her food into the garbage disposal. Her appetite had fled. Even the smell of the sour cream chocolate cake—her favorite—nauseated her.

Restless, she began washing dishes. A few minutes later, Jason laid a hand on her shoulder from behind. Her nerves shot, she jumped. A glass flew out of her soapy hands and shattered on the linoleum.

She couldn't contain her sobs any longer. "Why is he doing this? Why can't he leave me alone? I know God is protecting me, but I'm scared, Jason. What does this man want from me?"

He drew her close and stroked her hair. "I don't know. But I promise we'll find him."

"Do you think so?"

"Absolutely. Now, let's finish in here before Bruce and Abby arrive."

Jason swept up the glass while Jenna emptied the sink. By the time they'd tidied the kitchen, the doorbell rang.

Bruce and Abby gathered around the table in an obvious conference. "Who has Jenna's new phone number?" Jason asked.

"I gave it to three people—Abby, my boss, and you," Jenna said.

"I didn't tell anyone," Abby asserted.

"Neither did I. So that leaves Masters."

Jenna shook her head. "I don't believe he'd reveal it. He knows why I requested an unlisted number in the first place. He probably placed it in my file or laid it on his desk."

"Then we're back to someone either in or having access to your department. We've already eliminated your neighbors,"

Jason said.

"He claims you have something that doesn't belong to you," Bruce repeated, his brow furrowed in thought. "I wonder what it could be?"

"Maybe he's referring to something intangible," Abby blurted out.

Three pairs of eyes fixed on Abby's face. "What do you mean?" Bruce asked.

"Maybe it's an honor Jen's received, or a raise." Abby's face brightened. "Maybe it's her job. I heard competition was fierce. Someone may have thought he should have been the one they hired."

"Or promoted," Jason added. "How many of St. Anne's staff applied for the position?"

Abby shrugged. "Sam was interested in it. I'm sure there were others. John probably kept a file on all the candidates."

"I'll check it out." Jason reached over to grab Jenna's hand. "I want you to stay with Abby."

"I won't let him dictate my actions," Jenna said, stubbornly.

"Can you honestly tell me you'll sleep tonight?"

She fell silent. They both knew she wouldn't.

"Pack your things. If you won't go to Abby's, I'll take you to a hotel."

"It's just for one night. Right?"

"One night," Jason echoed. With any luck at all, Jenna's problems would soon be over.

❧

He sat in semi-darkness, watching twilight descend upon the neighborhood while reflecting on his day's work. The shadows cast on his face added another measure of evil to the already fiendish grin plastered there.

His new friend's cellular phone had worked perfectly from the block next to her house. From his parking spot near the bushes on a vacant lot, he could monitor her front yard without being seen. In fact, he knew the exact moment she'd left with her boyfriend.

Oh, he loved to hear the terror in the lofty Mrs. Carlson's voice. It wouldn't be long before he convinced her to pack her bags for good and go back where she came from.

❦

A few days later, Jason watched Jenna deep in a discussion with one of her staff. Her animated face had become so familiar. Their leisurely walks, bike rides, and the hours spent talking this past week, had given him such joy. He'd finally found the companionship he wanted.

Worries over adoption still plagued him from time to time, but he pushed them aside whenever he could. He'd have to address the issue before long, but for now he was content to let it ride. St. Anne's case was his top priority.

He wasn't certain if Jenna's attitudes had changed, but her questions about his work boded well. Although his job possessed a certain element of danger at times, he didn't dwell on the risks. Perhaps, Jenna would do the same.

Jason advanced, skirting people and equipment to reach Jenna's side. His news couldn't wait and his sixth sense forewarned him of her reaction. Her good day was about to turn into a bad one.

"Hello, Jason," she acknowledged before refocusing her attention on the notepad in her hand. "I'm sorry, but I can't take a break. I'm up to my eyelashes in blood samples."

"I'm not here for a break. I have to talk to you." He hesitated. "It's serious."

Her face blanched. She tossed the pad onto her desk and led the way into John's office.

"What's wrong?" she asked.

The facts couldn't be sugarcoated and he didn't try. "We arrested Sam this morning."

eleven

Jenna's jaw dropped and her eyes grew wide. "I don't believe it."

Jason crossed his arms. "It's true. We have plenty of evidence. Being his boss and friend, I thought you'd want to be the first to know. I imagine you'll be fielding a lot of questions."

She sank into a chair. "But, it can't be! I know Sam and his family. There has to be some mistake. You're saying he's been making those calls, stealing money and jewelry, planting it in my desk?"

He nodded.

"Sam isn't your man," she insisted.

"I know it's hard to accept, but we had no choice."

"What happens now?"

"It's up to the district attorney."

A minute of silence passed.

"I'm sorry, Jenna. We had to do it."

"What was his motive? Was he upset because I got the job?"

"Apparently."

"So Sam's the thief."

"It appears so."

She looked him straight in the eye. "You're wrong."

"I know you're defending your friend, but as I said earlier, we have the evidence."

"Have you told. . .does anyone else know about this?" Her voice shook.

"Payce will make the official announcement. He's probably doing it right now at the board meeting."

"I see. Thanks for telling me."

She fled with a thoughtful expression on her face. Although

131

she obviously had many doubts and unanswered questions, she'd have to accept the situation.

Yet, as he drove Jenna to the ball field that evening, she still seemed preoccupied. "You haven't said much tonight," he said.

She sighed. "I'm thinking."

"About Sam, right?"

"He isn't guilty."

"What makes you say that?"

"I'm basing it on a totally unscientific, illogical theory. It just doesn't feel right."

"I need concrete evidence, not your intuition," he reminded her.

"But haven't you ever been in a situation where things didn't click? That's how I feel about Sam."

"People often do surprising things."

"I suppose. But you need to keep looking."

"I won't turn down another suspect if one walks through the door. Okay?"

The next few hours passed quickly as Jenna's team won their game against the Walnut Bowl, eight to six. While St. Anne's players received congratulations, Jason gathered the equipment. Although no one was overtly rude, he sensed the displeasure emanating from Abby, Jenna, and the few others who knew Sam.

Shoving the bats into a bag, he overheard bits of a furtive conversation between Jenna, Abby, and two women whose names he couldn't remember. The words "necklace" and "trap" stopped him and he filled in the rest.

Those crazy women! All I need now is interference from a group of amateurs.

He didn't intend a stealthy approach, but they were too engrossed in their conspiracy to have heard a buffalo stampede. "I hope you're not thinking what I think you're thinking." He directed his deadly calm voice towards the person he considered to be the plot's instigator.

Utter silence. The look on their faces, Jenna's in particular, reminded him of a kid caught with his hand in a cookie jar.

Immediately, Jenna squared her shoulders and arched an eyebrow. "That depends on what you're thinking."

"Well," he drawled, "I think none of you agree Sam is the thief. Now you're concocting a plan to trap the real crook. Am I right?"

Jenna's tell-tale flush confirmed his theory. The others remained silent.

Jason fixed his gaze on Jenna. "Here's a news flash for you and for anyone else who might dream up another goofy idea. If any of you meddle in this investigation, you'll be in jail so fast your heads will spin. Do I make myself perfectly clear?"

Abby and the others murmured their understanding and fled. Jenna stood toe-to-toe with Jason. A long minute later, her shoulders slumped. "Yes."

"Let's go." Without giving her a chance to do or say anything else, he grabbed her elbow and guided her to his shiny black sports-utility vehicle—a newer version of his old one.

"I'm sorry I was sharp with you," he began once they were on the road back to her house. "But I had to be sure you ladies understand how serious it is to interfere in a major investigation. As much as I didn't like to read you the riot act, I had no choice.

"I understand your desire to help Sam. Your loyalty to him is commendable and I'm sure Sam would be thrilled to know of your support. But you have to trust me. I know what I'm doing."

Jenna's smile was wan. "I hope so, Jason. I certainly hope so."

"Do you know what you need?" he asked, turning left at the next intersection instead of right. She shook her head. "Ice cream," he replied. "As my Grandpa always said, 'It's good for what ails you'."

"Then by all means, let's go."

They stopped at an ice cream shop that enjoyed a booming business. Knowing her preference, he asked, "A sundae? Strawberry. Right?"

"Is there any other kind?"

While she found a picnic table, Jason stood in line for her sundae and his chocolate-dipped cone. Upon his return, he watched a young mother spoon ice cream into a toddler's mouth.

The little girl chortled with each bite, waving her hands in the air and bouncing up and down on her father's lap with excitement. When the treat was gone, her little chin quivered and her lower lip jutted out. "No more?" she asked.

"No more," her mother replied, wiping the small sticky face with a napkin.

The child opened her mouth to deliver an ear-crashing wail. Before a sound came forth, her father hoisted her up on his shoulders. "How about a ride, Cassie?"

Cassie latched onto his hair and giggled, the reason for her outrage already forgotten.

Jason watched the happy family walk down the street. Without any doubt, he wanted to be a part of a picture like that, with Jenna at his side. He glanced at Jenna, catching her wistful expression. "She's a cutie, isn't she?"

The corners of her mouth turned up slightly. "Yes, she is."

"I wonder if girls are messier than boys."

"Boys are much worse than girls. My nephews come home a lot dirtier than my nieces."

"Hey, now," he protested. "That sounds like a prejudiced remark."

"But it's true," she affirmed. "Boys like being grubby."

"Another stereotypical assumption," he returned without

rancor. Their banter continued until he parked in front of her house. As he accompanied her to the door, he decided to leave her with one last thought.

"Jenna," he began, caressing her cheek with his fingers. "I love you and I'd like nothing more than for us to get married. I've done a lot of thinking lately, and although I can't jump for joy when I consider adopting our children, I think I can be open-minded about it. Is that good enough?"

She bit her lip and fell silent. "I don't know, Jason," she finally said. "Now I'm the one who needs some time to think. And pray."

"You've got it," he promised, lowering his head to kiss her goodnight. "Sleep tight and I'll see you tomorrow."

☙

He threw the can across the room and watched the beer splash against the wall before running down in sticky rivers. It just wasn't fair.

He'd planned as many robberies as he could around Jenna's schedule, but Daly went and arrested someone else. Well, Mrs. Carlson just had to leave St. Anne's, and, one way or another, he'd make her.

☙

Still pondering Jason's comments, Jenna clocked in the next morning as was her routine. Once again she'd read the Psalms until the words blurred on the page, and she was exhausted.

As if mechanical gizmos sensed mental turmoil, her combination lock jammed on the first turn. Unable to open her locker after five minutes of wriggling, jiggling, and muttering, she telephoned the maintenance department for assistance.

Within ten minutes, the familiar Gerald and Harry arrived. "The dial won't turn so I can't open my locker," she reported. "I don't care what you do, just get the lock off."

"We may have to saw it in two," Gerald, a fortyish stockily-built fellow, warned.

"Fine. Do whatever it takes."

Harry found her fifteen minutes later. "Here you go," he said, dropping two metal scraps in her hand.

"Thanks. I'll replace it tonight."

She left her extra lab coat inside, but kept her purse in her possession. *No sense providing temptation,* she thought. She never carried too much cash but she'd rather not lose her two credit cards.

Plagued by uncertainty over Jason's suggestion, she silently thanked God for his guidance throughout the morning. Although she didn't have an answer as yet, her faith told her one would be forthcoming.

Abby was sympathetic when Jenna spilled her story over lunch. "I understand your dilemma, my friend, but you have to ask yourself, are you happier with him or without him? And don't consider any 'what ifs' because no one knows the future."

Abby's question echoed through Jenna's mind throughout the remainder of the day. By the time her shift ended, she'd made a decision.

Intending to grab a tissue from the box in her locker, she was surprised to find two small packages, each addressed with her name, inside.

Ripping the wrapping paper off the smallest one first, she flipped open the padded box to discover a half-carat diamond solitaire nestled inside.

Astonished, she tore into the second package. It contained a woman's gold watch, its face encrusted with diamonds.

Oh, Jason, she thought, tenderly. As she admired the expensive articles, a foreboding suddenly spread through her. She didn't recognize the ring, but the watch looked familiar. In fact, she'd seen a similar one in a patient's room and had complimented the owner on its design. But Jason had arrested the thief, hadn't he?

She stuffed the jewelry into her pocket and made a beeline

down the hallway.

Pushing her way past a startled Bruce and his secretary, Jenna marched into Jason's temporary office. He smiled a greeting, but his delighted expression soon changed to alarm. "What's wrong?"

"I. . .I. . ." Words failed her. She removed the jewelry from her pocket and began again. "I found these in my locker. At first I thought you sent them, but then. . ." Her voice died on a quavery note.

Jason skirted the desk, guided her to a chair, then tugged the items from her cold, lifeless fingers.

Wordlessly he handed them to the security director who'd followed her into the office. "You're right. These were stolen."

"Oh, no." Her voice shook.

"Do you recognize this watch?"

"Yes. It belongs to Mrs. Montgomery, room 448."

"Do you remember a Ms. Taylor in room 446?"

"Vaguely. I drew blood from the patients on that wing this morning. Is the ring hers?"

Jason nodded. "Any ideas on how he got into your locker?"

She pulled two mangled pieces of metal from her pocket. "The dial jammed and two maintenance men sawed it off." A thought occurred to her and with it came relief. "This proves Sam isn't your man. He hasn't been at work since he was suspended."

Jason hunkered down, taking her hand in his. "Are you absolutely certain you don't know of anyone who has reason to frame you, Jenna?"

"I'm positive."

"Okay." Jason's people were still pursuing Abby's job angle. They had eliminated St. Anne's staff, but were continuing their investigation on the remaining applicants. It seemed unbelievable that anyone would go to this much trouble if he or she was presently employed. Only one candidate didn't have a job, and she was caring for an elderly parent in Wisconsin.

Jason looked at Bruce. "Your man didn't report anyone suspicious in those two rooms?"

"The only ones who went in were nursing staff, the physician, Jenna, and two maintenance men."

"You mean. . .this was a trap? And you didn't tell me?" Her voice ended on a squeak.

"We kept it quiet for two reasons. We'd hoped that by announcing Sam was the thief, the real one would become careless. We needed you to stick to your routine and act as normal as possible."

"You still should have warned me," she chided.

He grinned. "No offense, but don't play poker. Your face, as beautiful as it is, is too expressive. Be honest. If you had known we'd planted the jewelry with those patients, you wouldn't have stormed down here like you did."

"Probably not," she admitted. "By the way, those fake diamonds looked so real."

"Who said anything about fake?" At her gasp, he continued, "Luckily, our thief gives his goods to you. It made it easier for Payce to approve our scheme."

"So, now what happens?"

"We wait and watch. Each day, a special list of 'patients' will be given to you and you'll do what you normally do. It shouldn't take too long to catch him in the act."

"And Sam?"

"Sam is on a paid vacation, which by the way, thrilled him to pieces."

Jenna's eyes shone and she hugged him. "Oh, Jason, this is wonderful."

He embraced her longer than necessary. "I told you to trust me," he whispered, for her ears only. "Now don't you feel rotten for having such little faith?"

Her face warmed. "I suppose so."

"In the meantime," Jason warned, "Don't tell anyone about Sam."

"I won't."

He pointed her toward the door. "Bruce and I have some work to finish. I'll see you later."

Leaving the hospital, she rejoiced in her friend's innocence. Yet, she had a sobering thought. She still didn't know who had a vendetta against her.

Later that evening, she heard footsteps and caught a glimpse of a tall form on the wooden porch. Thinking Jason had arrived, she was surprised when she didn't hear his familiar knock. She turned toward the door just as the living room's picture window shattered. Something stung her arm.

A brick lay on the floor at her feet. The episode took on surreal proportions as someone rattled the doorknob.

Panic struck. Someone was trying to get inside!

twelve

Isaiah's verse immediately flashed into Jenna's mind. *No weapon formed against me shall prosper.* Buoyed by the thought, she dashed to the closet, pulled out a baseball bat, and poised herself to strike.

Every sound, both inside and outside, seemed magnified, but after several long minutes, the noises were ones she'd heard a thousand times before—the honk of a distant car horn, the chug-chug of yard sprinklers, the mailman's whistled tune.

She relaxed. The tread of feet on her porch sounded once again and once again, she tensed for action.

The doorbell rang. Should she answer?

"Jenna. Jenna. Are you in there?"

The baritone was blessedly familiar. She opened the door and dropped the bat in her rush to find comfort in Jason's arms.

"What happened?" he asked.

She clutched his shirt front with both hands. "He was here. He threw that brick inside and then he rattled the door. I thought he was coming in!"

Fifteen minutes later, the police arrived. Jenna repeated her story, while Jason tended the superficial cut on her arm.

Feeling cold in spite of the ninety-five degree heat, she watched the officers examine her window. They walked the neighborhood to search for clues and at Jason's insistence, they checked the vacant house across the street.

They didn't find anything suspicious.

"Pack some clothes," Jason said. "I'm taking you to Abby's. You can't stay here tonight."

Meekly, Jenna complied. Staying alone wasn't appealing. It also wasn't an idea she'd consider.

"Is it ever going to end, Jason?" she asked.

"It will. I promise." With that he kissed her. "I'll be by in the morning to take you to work, so don't leave without me."

"It's too early. You don't have to go in until eight."

"If you think I'm going to stay in bed while you're driving the streets at six in the morning, you'd better think again. Besides, we always put in whatever hours it takes when we're close to solving a case."

"All right."

True to his word, Jason arrived by six A.M. After such a short night, he appeared more lively than she felt.

"Whenever you leave the lab, pay close attention to each person you see or deal with," he ordered. "I also have several operatives who'll be nearby, blending into the woodwork, so to speak. If you need help, yell. Don't be heroic. Whatever you do, today, act normal."

"I'll try."

He escorted her to the laboratory, looking as if this day was like all the others. Underneath his cheerful and relaxed façade, however, she noticed his vigilance. Every person who crossed their path underwent his scrutiny.

He chose to work at the conference room table for its unobstructed view of her desk. Documents spilled out of his open briefcase and corroborated the "investigation" story he had circulated.

Although his presence alleviated her fears, it hadn't totally banished the threat posed by the anonymous caller. Although she preferred to stay in the relative safety of the lab, she forced herself to stick to her routine.

At two o'clock, Jason suggested a coffee break in the cafeteria. While they served themselves at the beverage counter, several men from the maintenance department surrounded them.

"Hi Jenna. Any more lock problems?"

"Hello, Gerald. No, my new padlock works great. I appreciate your help."

"No problem. By the way, congratulations. I read about you softball victory in the hospital's newsletter. It's nice to see a trophy for St. Anne's."

"Isn't it? I understand Payce authorized a display case to be built in the hospital lobby. You men need to earn one to keep ours company!" she teased.

"Just wait until next year," Gerald promised.

Jenna handed the clerk the exact change before finding an unoccupied table. Jason dallied at the soda fountain, hoping to speak with Gerald a little longer since he had sawed off Jenna's tampered lock. His patience was rewarded.

"Jenna is quite a gal," Gerald mentioned as he filled his cup with ice. "You're a lucky man."

"I think so," Jason replied.

"Yup, there were a lot of disappointed fellows around the hospital when she took up with you. Not that she didn't make a good choice," Gerald hastened to add, "but a lot of guys kept hoping, if you know what I mean."

Jason grinned and nodded.

"Why, we have a fellow working with us that has such a crush on her, he knocks himself out trying to get assigned to her department. Poor kid." Gerald shook his head. "He has it bad."

"Oh, really? Who is this guy? It doesn't hurt to size up the competition." Jason looked up and down the serving line, scrutinizing every male in a tan maintenance uniform. His senses jumped to full alert. This could be his long overdue break.

"He's off today, but don't worry. He's just a kid—about twenty. If Jenna didn't notice him before, she certainly won't now. Name's Austin. Harry Austin."

"Thanks. Take it easy." Jason paid for his drink and strode toward Jenna's table. "Do you know a Harry Austin?" he asked her.

"Austin." Jenna thought a moment. "I know a Lydia Austin, but not a Harry. Am I supposed to?"

"Your friend Gerald said this fellow has a crush on you."

"Really? I'm flattered." She sipped her orange drink through the straw.

"Don't let it go to your head," he growled.

Jenna's mouth twitched. "Surely you don't think *he* is behind this, do you? A boy with a crush wouldn't set someone up as a thief, would he?"

"Who knows? Stranger things have happened."

❧

That same evening, Jason hurried home in order to keep his appointment with his neighbors' social worker.

"How do the Farleys treat their two children?" Susan Hill asked.

"They spend a lot of time with them. Tom and Sally take an active role in their school activities, too."

"Have you every suspected or seen any signs of abuse?"

"No. Never."

The social worker's questions continued, but by the end of the interview, he suspected Tom and Sally wouldn't have any trouble adding a youth to their household. Once the social worker's official business concluded, Jason sought his own answers.

"By the way, how long does it take to adopt a baby? I understand the waiting list is long."

"Yes, it is. We consider a number of factors before approving a couple. Things like their age, attitude, stability, etc. are important issues."

Jason relayed his niece's story.

Susan sighed. "Unfortunately the situation you described does occur. Not often, thank goodness, but mistakes do happen. People aren't infallible." She dug in her purse. "Here's my card, in case you ever need it."

Jason showed her to the door, his mind racing with everything from possibilities to the old doubts and fears. Could he risk heartbreak like Carolyn and Mark and countless other couples in order to have a family?

❧

The next morning, Jason willed the phone to ring. After sending his subordinates to find Harry Austin last night, he was impatient for their report. His first legitimate suspect wouldn't slip through his fingers.

"Phone call, Mr. Daly."

Jason snatched up the receiver and listened to Burrows' briefing. "Thanks. Keep someone there in case he shows."

"Will do," Burrows said.

An idea formed. "Hey, wait a minute." Jason paused to rifle through an opened file. "He lists his sister as next-of-kin. Maybe he's there."

Jason read the address before breaking the phone connection. He tried to fit the newest piece into the puzzle. Harry's sister was Lydia—a woman both Jenna and Bruce knew. Was the acquaintance a connection or a coincidence?

Bruce strode through the doorway. "Good morning," he said cheerfully.

"I think we have our man," Jason said.

"No kidding? Who?"

"Harry Austin. His next-of-kin lists his sister, Lydia."

Bruce's jaw dropped. "Tell me you're joking."

"I wish."

"Lydia's mentioned him, but we've never been introduced. How did he become a suspect?"

"According to one of his fellow employees, Harry's been asking a lot of questions about Jenna. Rumor says he has a crush on her."

"Maybe."

Jason shook his head. "Considering what's been going on, the story sounds more like a cover to keep tabs on her. Other things fit, too. He has access everywhere in the hospital—any time, any place. The question is, what's his motive? Why did he single out Jenna? And why has he suddenly disappeared?"

"He has?"

"We can't find him at home or at work. According to his boss, he requested vacation time for a few days, but no one knows where he might have gone."

Bruce frowned. "That's odd. Lydia's been trying to reach him, too."

Jason slammed the file closed after pulling out a photo. "If he left town for a little R and R, we'll have to wait until he returns. While I check on Jenna, why don't you see what you can learn from Lydia?"

❧

Jenna fretted. Staff were pressuring her for supplies and Jason hadn't arrived. She'd never asked anyone to accompany her to the storeroom before, so it would seem odd if she did so now. Unable to postpone her responsibilities any longer, she decided to ignore his directive. List in hand, she wheeled the cart through the back hallway which connected the laboratory and radiology, and unlocked the door.

She flicked on the light switch. One of the bulbs sputtered, then went dark. Reminding herself to report it as soon as she returned, she pushed the cart through the aisles of stacked goods, selecting those checked on her form.

A young maintenance man stepped out of the shadows to stand before her. She jumped, shaken by his unexpected appearance. "Oh, Harry. You scared me."

"Sorry. The air-conditioner unit is malfunctioning."

"One of the lights at the other end burned out, too. Can you replace it since you're here?" she asked.

"Sure."

Jenna grabbed her last item, then left the storeroom without a backward glance.

An hour later, Jason perched on the edge of Jenna's desk. "What's so funny? Anything exciting happen this morning?"

Jenna grinned. "No. I'm just planning to tease Bill, the maintenance supervisor, the next time I see him."

"Why?"

"I ran into one of his men in our storeroom this morning—"

"You did what? You know you aren't to go anywhere without me!"

"I know, but I had people hounding me for supplies and I couldn't wait. Anyway, Harry didn't even have a screwdriver and he supposedly was fixing the air-conditioner. I can hear Bill now," she faked a gruff voice, "my people have to diagnose the problem before they bring their equipment."

"Harry?" The gleam in Jason's eyes and his clipped tone made goose bumps rise on Jenna's forearms.

"Yeah, Harry. You've seen him in here before."

He removed a photograph from his shirt pocket and handed it to her. "Is this the Harry you're referring to?"

She glanced at the unflattering employee mugshot of a men in his early twenties with light brown hair. "That's him."

"You're positive."

"Absolutely." He yanked the walkie-talkie off of his belt—a walkie-talkie she'd never seen in his possession before.

"What's wrong?" she asked.

He didn't answer, speaking instead to someone on the radio. "He's here. Last seen on the main floor between the lab and x-ray." He signed off and replaced the unit on his belt.

"You think Harry's the one, don't you?"

"Yes."

"How can you be so sure?"

"Remember how we set up a number of rooms and monitored everyone who went inside? In each case, one man from maintenance also stopped by after you did. Always Austin."

"So?"

"Jenna," Jason said gently, "we checked. There weren't any maintenance problems reported concerning those rooms. He didn't have a reason to be there."

"But he's always been so polite, so helpful. It doesn't seem likely for him to threaten me."

"What better way to throw you off his trail? Now, if only we can locate him before he realizes we're on to his tricks."

"If he's working, he shouldn't be hard to find."

"According to his boss, he's officially on vacation. Since you saw him a short time ago, that means he doesn't want anyone to know he's here. Until we nab him, don't leave the lab. If you do, be sure someone's with you, preferably me, Bruce, or one of my people."

If Jason's theory was correct, she'd been in terrible danger and hadn't realized it. A cold chill descended and she rubbed at the goosebumps on her arms. "I won't."

He rose. After pulling her to her feet, he tugged her behind the nearest support pillar. There, he held her for a few seconds before he kissed her. "Don't worry."

She managed a weak smile. "I'll try not to."

He reluctantly drew away. She was equally reluctant to release him. "See you later," he said. "Be careful."

"I will." Jenna returned to her desk. Although she tried to immerse herself in the latest quality assurance monitors, her concentration strayed and she blamed her inattention on the tense situation.

What was the name Jason used? Austin, that was it. Satisfied she'd remembered, its familiarity hit her. Was he related to Lydia Austin, Bruce's girlfriend?

ع

Jason stormed into the security offices moments after he'd left Jenna. "Have you located him yet?"

Bruce shook his head. "He knows every hidey-hole in this hospital. Lydia is checking his apartment."

"Well, we have to find him."

The secretary knocked on the door. "Excuse me, Bruce. There's a woman here who insists on seeing you."

"Did she say why? Can she make an appointment for another day?"

"She's very adamant." Monica referred to a small note in her hand. "Her name is Lydia Austin."

Bruce jumped to his feet, staring at the other man. "Send her in. And hold all calls."

Monica showed Lydia into the room and eased the door closed.

Bruce took her hand and led her to a chair. "What's wrong?"

Lydia clenched the purse on her lap. "I went to Harry's house right after you called. I found a wad of bills and a lot of jewelry piled on a dresser. The pieces looked too expensive for him to buy." She hesitated before continuing in a quivery voice. "I think he's your thief."

Bruce laid a hand on her shoulder. "I'm sorry you had to find out this way."

Jason felt the couple's pain. Harry's actions had touched a

lot of innocent people. Being involved in obtaining evidence to throw his fiancée's brother in jail wouldn't help Bruce's romance. And Lydia's agony was just beginning. It couldn't have been easy to come forward with her suspicions, and he respected her decision to do what was morally and ethically correct regardless of family ties.

However, his concern for Jenna overshadowed all else. Sympathy could wait until Harry was behind bars.

Her mouth trembled. "When did you suspect my brother?"

Jason answered. "Yesterday."

"I see."

"We're trying to find Harry right now—to ask him a few questions," Bruce said.

She nodded. "He's supposed to be on medication, but his prescription bottle hasn't been touched."

"Medication? What sort of medication?" Jason asked.

"I forget what it's called. Dr. Lee would know. Dr. Janice Lee."

He exchanged a glance with Bruce. "The psychiatrist?"

She nodded. "When you find him, would you please take that under consideration, and call his doctor?" She pulled a slip of paper out of her skirt pocket.

Bruce took the scrap and handed it to Jason. "I hope we're wrong, Lydia. But I'm glad you came."

She rose, slinging her purse over one shoulder. "I hope I'm wrong too, but I don't think I am."

Jason stopped her. "We think he's trying to frame Jenna for some sort of revenge. Has he ever mentioned her or been in contact with her?"

"Jenna Carlson?" Lydia shook her head. "No, he's never said a word about her."

"What would he have against Jenna? What's his motive?"

Jason mused aloud. Suddenly, he clicked his fingers. "You're a medical technologist, too, aren't you, Lydia?"

"Y-yes."

"Did you by any chance, apply for the opening in the lab about six months ago?"

"I filled out a form, but I received a promotion at St. Mark's, so I withdrew my application. Why?"

"Just curious." That explained why her name wasn't on Masters' interview list. "Did Harry seem unhappy because you didn't come to St. Anne's?"

"He wasn't overjoyed when I told him I wasn't changing hospitals. He knew how much I wanted a day shift position, but we needed the extra money from the shift differential. Psychiatrists aren't cheap and Harry's health insurance doesn't cover everything."

Her eyes grew troubled. "Are you saying Harry is stealing things because I don't work here?"

"It's possible," Jason prevaricated.

"But that doesn't make sense," she protested, then stopped herself. "Forget I said that. Harry doesn't process information like the rest of us. It's all my fault," she chastised herself, unshed tears glistening in her sad eyes.

"You aren't responsible for his decisions," Bruce said vehemently.

Lydia swallowed and jumped to her feet. "Yes, well, if you'll excuse me. . ." She rushed out of the room.

"Lydia, wait," Bruce called, but she didn't look back.

"We have our motive," Jason stated.

"No wonder the guy harped on Jenna having something that wasn't hers. Harry believed the job belonged to his sister, even though she didn't want it."

"Exactly. And if his mental illness is no longer controlled by medication. . ." Jason's voice faded. "Keep your men looking for Austin. Monitor the exits. Enlist every available person if necessary, but *I want him found!*"

Jason strode down the hall to lab with one thought running through his mind. *O God, keep her safe.*

thirteen

Jenna cocked her head to hold the receiver on her shoulder while she signed a leave request. "Abby, we're swamped over here today. Would you mind waiting until three o'clock to pick up your inventory forms? I should have them ready by then."

"Okay. See you at three."

Jenna hung up. The workload had escalated during the past few hours to the point she couldn't afford to let her mind wander. Praying Jason would find Harry Austin soon so Sam could return to his duties, she helped the tech at the profiling analyzer.

Once the instrument spat out the last patient result, Jenna looked up the missing cost figures and jotted the numbers on the master inventory list. At two forty-five, one of the clerks approached her.

"A patient in room 641 needs a glucose drawn at 3:00 P.M. and I don't have anyone to send."

Jenna scanned her department. Her harried coworkers were scurrying to complete their assignments and she hated to add another task to their burden. "I'll take care of it, Eileen," she sighed. She wasn't exactly twiddling her thumbs either, but patients took precedence over paperwork.

She dialed Jason's extension and heard a busy signal. Opting to page him, time inched closer to three and he hadn't returned her call. Having no other choice, she decided to go alone. After all, she'd made it to the supply room and back in one piece, even after running into Harry. Besides, Jason's people were hanging around. If she got into trouble, all she had to do was yell.

At 2:55, Jenna grabbed a tray from the phlebotomy area and reminded the clerks of her destination. "Be sure you tell Mr. Daly where I am if he arrives or telephones before I get back."

Room 641's door opened without a sound and she noted the empty bed and closed bathroom. Surmising the patient was using the facilities, she assembled her equipment and laid a pair of latex gloves on the table.

By 3:00 P.M., her patient hadn't appeared. Concerned, Jenna knocked on the door. "Mrs. Potter, are you in there?"

The door swung outward and Jenna gasped. Harry—the young man she'd always thought so friendly—stood in the frame.

"Excuse me." Jenna hoped she didn't sound as nervous as she felt. "I thought my patient was in there."

"No, just me and a broken sink."

Harry's eyes held a cold, calculating quality—one she'd never seen before. Her scalp tingled and all the comments Jason had made came screaming back. *We think he's the one. He's officially on vacation. No one's been able to locate him.*

"I'll check with the nurses' station and see where she is. Sorry to interrupt you." Jenna tried to snatch the lab carryall from the bedside table, but as she reached for it, he grabbed her from behind.

"You know who I am, don't you?" he rasped in her ear.

His arm encircled her throat. Jenna attempted to loosen his hold in order to breath and discovered an unlikely weapon in one hand. Somehow, she'd snatched the blood collection system off the table.

"What do you want?" she choked out.

"I want what belongs to my sister," he intoned.

"I don't understand. What are you talking about?" She tried to be calm but her heart pounded and her vision dimmed as her air supply dwindled.

"You stole the job away from my sister. She deserved it, not you. Your boyfriend is on to me, so you're my hostage, my ticket out of here." He dragged her toward the door, keeping his left arm pressed against her windpipe.

She dug her fingernails into his forearm. *Think, Jenna, think!* Maneuvering the tube system in her right hand, she pushed the hard protective cap off the needle with her thumb and saw it arc to the floor. She wondered if he heard the faint noise, then decided it didn't matter.

Without hesitation, she buried the needle in his muscular forearm. Grunting with pain, he loosened his grip just enough for Jenna to break free. She dashed into the hallway.

A bang sounded near her head and she ducked. *He had a gun?* she thought, amazed, dodging into the nearest exit. It was a good thing she hadn't known before she tried her stunt. Her puny needle was no match for a speeding bullet.

She hustled down the stairs. People. She had to get out of the stairwell and surround herself with people. He wouldn't find her in a crowd.

Turning the corner, she heard another ping. *Where are Jason's men?*

Jenna reached the fifth floor and burst through the doors. Of all times, the normally bustling hallway was deserted.

Glancing over one shoulder, she saw Harry come through the stairwell opening. Spurred on by his proximity, she ran past the nurses' station to the exit at the other end of the ward. She lost her footing and tripped down the rough concrete stairs, landing on her hands and knees.

Palms scraped, knees throbbing, she wheezed for a few seconds. The metal fire door at the top of the stairs banged against the wall.

Afraid to waste time looking over her shoulder to verify Austin's approach, she scrambled to her feet and hurried down another flight. The fourth floor exit appeared, but hoping to fool him, she bypassed it. Rushing down to the third floor, she heard the now-familiar report of his weapon. It sounded closer. Unversed in guns, she wondered if it was a forty-five. Not that it mattered, dead was dead.

O God, please let me straighten out the situation with Jason!

She felt a stitch in her side, attributing it to failing stamina. Once again, no one was available to help and she couldn't wait for someone to appear. Where *was* everybody? She ran through the hall and dashed into the opposite stairwell. Panting, she paused a few seconds to catch her breath.

Suddenly she understood what Abby had been telling her all along—accidents, violence, and death weren't limited to professions like Chad's or Jason's.

The seedier side of life spilled over into everything. No job was immune. Not even hers.

❧

Abby waited at Jenna's desk until 3:30, then meandered to the office area. "Where did you say Jenna went?"

Eileen answered. "Sixth floor for a three o'clock glucose. Isn't she back yet?"

Abby drummed her fingers on the counter. "No, she's not. I wonder if she's having trouble."

The phone rang. Eileen answered and her eyes widened. She beckoned to Abby as she spoke to the person on the telephone. "I don't know what to tell you. I sent someone to take Mrs. Potter's blood sample before three o'clock. Are you absolutely certain?"

Eileen paused, listening. "I'll send someone else right away," she promised before she broke the connection.

"What happened?"

"The nurses say a lab tray is in the room, but no one's there. Mrs. Potter insists the room was empty when she returned from x-ray."

Fear coursed through Abby. One of the first things lab students learned was to never, ever, leave their equipment unattended in a patient room. For Jenna to do so meant she was in trouble. Big trouble.

"Send someone to collect the tray and take care of the patient."

She crashed through the doors into the hallway and nearly mowed down Jason. "Thank God, it's you! Jenna is missing!"

"She's what?" he thundered.

"We can't find her. She went to sixth floor—her tray is in the room—but the nursing staff say she never saw the patient."

Jason's heart sank. Jenna was in trouble, his instincts said so. He yanked the walkie-talkie off his belt and spoke. "Get extra men at every exit and don't let Austin out of here. Look for Mrs. Carlson, too. We can't locate her."

Abby's face grew pale. "Austin? Who are you talking about? What's going on?"

"Harry Austin is our thief and the one who's been harassing Jenna. She saw him earlier, but he's not on duty. He probably suspects we've caught on and now he's desperate."

"Oh, no."

Jason headed for the hallway. "A few prayers wouldn't hurt right now. If she shows up, page me."

He jogged to the elevator, brushing past staff and visitors alike in his haste. *Keep her in the shadow of your wings, Lord.*

He met Bruce outside room 641. A telltale scratch on the metal door frame caught his eye and he pointed it out to his partner.

"It looks like she got away and he shot at her," Jason remarked, trying to stay objective. "She probably headed for these stairs since it's the nearest exit."

Jason inspected the door casing. "Here's another mark. Send

your people to each floor and find out if anyone noticed or heard anything unusual."

Bruce spoke into his field radio and a few moments later, answers to Jason's request trickled over the air waves.

"Two nurses on the third and fifth floors have reported a popping noise coming from the hallway, but when they went to check it out, no one was there," Bruce stated.

"We know Jenna made it down three flights, probably heading for the lab. If we find her, I'm sure Austin won't be far behind," Jason said, his voice grim.

All of his reservations concerning his and Jenna's future together paled in comparison to the idea of losing her to a madman. Without a doubt, he wanted Jenna at his side—in sickness and in health, in good times and in bad.

Let her be safe, God.

Jason returned to the lab while Bruce journeyed to the third floor. At Abby's inquisitive look, Jason shook his head. "Have you told Masters about this?"

"Not yet."

He left Abby at the door while he searched for Jenna's superior. Discovering him in his office, he summarized the last few hours and secured Masters' promise to keep the information under wraps to avoid a panic.

Jason slipped out another exit, vowing to search every inch of the hospital, if necessary.

❧

Jenna reached the first floor, thanks to adrenaline and determination. Her whole body was bathed in a cold sweat.

She spied the gift shop and darted inside. Slowing to a walk, she hid behind a row of tall shelves filled with stuffed animals. A small space between two puppies was wide enough to allow her a view through the store's windows. From her position, she could see the elevators, the stairwell door, the hospital's lobby, and main entrance without being noticed. If her assailant followed her, she'd know it.

"May I help you?" a gray-headed pink lady volunteer asked.

Jenna's hand shook as she replaced a teddy bear on its shelf. "I'm just looking."

"If you need any help, just let me know."

"Thanks. I will." In the next instant, she came to a decision. "Actually, there is something you can do. Call security and ask for Mr. Daly. . ."

Her voice caught in her throat. Austin had entered the lobby via the stairwell entrance. She drew back, attempting to stay out of sight, yet wanting to see what he would do, where he would go. Where were the cops when you needed them?

"What did you want me to tell Mr. Daly, honey?" the little old lady asked.

Austin glanced in her direction and she drew back. His attention turned toward the elevator.

"Tell him Jenna was here." With that, she slipped out of the gift shop while the maintenance man's back faced her. Praying he wouldn't turn for the three seconds she needed to duck into the side hallway, she sprinted the few steps and stumbled into a restroom.

Luckily it was designed for single use and boasted a deadbolt latch for privacy. She slammed it home, depressed the lock button on the doorknob and sagged against the wall.

Her body shook as her adrenaline high disappeared. The stitch in her side nearly took her breath away and she pressed her hand against it.

She felt something wet, warm, and sticky. Blood covered her palm.

I've been shot, she thought, dumbfounded.

Thankful the restroom had a paper towel dispenser instead of a hot-air dryer, she yanked several paper towels out of the holder. Moving cautiously, she tugged her scrub top out of her pants and surveyed the damage.

Blood ran down the straight line running across her skin. It was deep and would require stitches, but only the fleshy part seemed to be injured. She pressed the makeshift bandage to the area and held it in place.

Lightheaded, she sank to the floor, rested her head against the wall, and closed her eyes.

❧

Bruce walked into the lab. "Is she here?" he asked a worried Abby.

"You haven't found her yet?" Abby shrieked.

He contacted Jason with his radio, then signed off. "I'm checking out E.R." He strode away, leaving Abby to pace the floor alone.

❧

Having received the volunteer's succinct message, Jason raced to the lobby. He arrived in time to see two of St. Anne's security officers subdue and slap handcuffs on an uncooperative Harry Austin. With Harry in custody, Jenna became his next priority. He hurried into the gift shop.

"I'm Jason Daly. I understand Jenna is here." He craned his neck to find her. "Where—"

"I made the call," the five-foot-nothing white-haired lady said. "She asked me to phone you, but then she disappeared."

Jason rubbed the back of his neck. "Did you see where she went?"

"I'm sorry, young man, but no, I didn't."

He met the officers as they were leaving the lobby. Giving Austin his most threatening glare, he demanded, "Where is she?"

"I don't know, and if I did I wouldn't tell you."

Jason's patience ended. He grabbed Austin by the lapels of

his uniform, lifted him to his feet, and thrust him against the wall.

Austin raised his handcuffed wrists to protect himself.

"I'm only going to say this once more," Jason ground out. "Where is Jenna?"

"I don't know. I lost her."

"If she's hurt. . ." Jason didn't finish his threat. Satisfied with the fear in the man's eyes, he released Austin's shirt as if it were something distasteful.

One of the guards displayed a revolver. "We found this on him."

The sight of the weapon infuriated Jason. The thought of Jenna lying injured, or dead, was too painful to contemplate. He clenched his fists, wanting dearly to smash Austin's face. With sheer strength of will, he restrained himself. "Get him out of here."

The two burly hospital guards led St. Anne's "ghost" to the security offices. Meanwhile, Jason ran his fingers through his dark hair. *Lord, where is she?*

Bruce cleared a path through the excited bystanders to reach Jason. "Any luck?"

"None. Austin said he lost her." He paused near the gift shop entrance and viewed the scene from his position. "We know she asked the volunteer to call me. Most likely, she saw Austin and ran again." He pointed. "This hallway links with the corridor leading to her department, doesn't it?"

"Yes."

Jason moved forward, poking his head into the cubicles they passed. Finally, he halted near two doors marked "Restroom" and pushed the first one open. It was empty.

Bruce tried the second door. The knob wouldn't turn.

Jason waved him aside, then pounded with his fist. "Security. Is anyone in here?"

The silence spoke for itself.

"I'll see if I can round up a key," Bruce offered.

Jason rattled the knob again. "Jenna? Are you in there?"

fourteen

Jenna opened her eyes. Had someone called her name, or had she imagined it? She listened, but didn't hear a thing.

Her watch read 4:30 P.M. It didn't seem like an hour and a half had elapsed, but it obviously had. She couldn't hide in the restroom forever. *Where is Jason?* she thought.

Debating the merits of lingering in her safe haven versus hunting for Jason herself, the ache in her side intensified. To her relief, the bleeding had slowed to an ooze.

She splashed water on her face and drank from her cupped hands. Somewhat revived although her legs were shaky, she hugged the wall on her way to the door.

Her fingers shook as she struggled to force the bolt back. Suddenly, a key grated in the lock. The button popped out; the knob turned.

She gasped and instinctively stepped backward. Releasing the deadbolt was out of the question.

The door rattled. "Jenna, are you in there?"

"Jason?" she whispered. Realizing he hadn't heard her, she rushed forward and repeated his name in a stronger voice. "Jason? Is that you?"

"Jenna, are you all right? Everyone's been looking for you! Can you open the door?"

She rattled the steel rod, but it barely moved a quarter of an inch. "The bolt's stuck." Tears of both frustration and relief burned her eyes.

"Keep trying."

Obeying his command, the rod moved another fraction.

Finally, it shot back with a sharp crack and a second later, the door swung open. Jason, with Bruce behind him, stood tall and straight before her.

Jenna smiled weakly at him. "You can't imagine how glad I am to see you." Without warning, her knees buckled.

Jason caught her. "Yes, I can. I've been worried sick."

His body heat felt like a warm blanket, and she felt herself drifting away. From a distance she heard him say something about blood and tried to reassure him. "It's only a scratch," she murmured before the darkness claimed her.

❧

Something held her hands. Had she hurt them without realizing it? Her eyelids fluttered open. Jason sat in a chair close to the bed, her hands resting in his.

Jason rose, then leaned over the gurney. "How are you feeling?"

She mentally took stock of her aches and pains. Only her side seemed to throb. "Not too bad."

"You're in E.R."

"I thought so." She licked her lips.

Anticipating her request, he held a glass of water near her chin.

"You're a lucky girl," he said while she sipped the water through the bendable straw. "The bullet traveled along your ribs. Other than the fifteen stitches Dr. Edison gave you, you're fine. You can go home as soon as you're ready."

"Did you find Harry? He was in the room waiting for me and I stuck him with my needle to get away. Then he started shooting—it was awful." She closed her eyes. "You did catch him, didn't you?"

"Yes, we did."

Now that she'd started telling her story, she couldn't stop. "He chased me through the hospital and I fell down the stairs.

When I made it to first floor, I had the lady call you. Did she call you? I wanted to wait for you, but then I saw him so I hid in the restroom. You did get him, didn't you?"

Jason brushed the hair off her forehead. "He's in jail. Don't worry, everything's all right."

She relaxed under his comforting ministrations and soothing tone.

The curtain rustled and Dr. Edison walked through. "Young lady," the gray-haired physician said in mock censure, "if you're trying to single-handedly raise our workman's compensation rates, you're doing a fine job."

Jenna offered a weak smile. "It looks that way, doesn't it? Don't worry, as much as I like your bedside manner, I don't want to come back."

"Jason tells me someone will be watching over you for the next few days. If that's the case, I'll release you."

Puzzled, she stared at Jason. "Did you call Abby?"

"She's on her way," he said.

As if on cue, a nurse arrived to help Jenna into a wheelchair and push her toward the emergency room entrance. Outside the double doors, she saw Bruce and Abby standing on the sidewalk near Jason's four-by-four.

Surrounded by friends in warm, welcoming sunshine, Jenna felt as if she'd awakened from a nightmare. Birds chirped, horns honked, and people went about their normal business. However, the gauze taped to her side attested to how unusual the day had really been. She shivered.

Jason bent over her. "Are you cold?"

She shook her head, reveling in the early evening's ninety-degree temperature. "I'm just glad to see you guys."

Abby looked misty-eyed.

"Bruce? When you see Lydia, tell her it's okay," Jenna said. "She's not responsible."

"I will," Bruce promised. "Provided she'll see me again. She's upset and embarrassed and I imagine she expects to deal with this all alone." He grinned. "Not unlike another woman I know."

Jenna smiled. "Don't let her get away with it."

"It's time to go," Jason interrupted. "We're blocking traffic." He lifted her into the passenger seat and fastened the seat belt before he slammed the door. Sliding behind the wheel, he buckled up, then pulled away from the curb.

Jenna studied Jason. His hair was ruffled and tension lines marred his features. She wanted to tell him of her decision, but decided to wait. Her announcement required his full attention.

"Where are we going?" she said instead.

"Home."

"Isn't Abby coming?"

"Later."

His clipped replies were puzzling, but she dismissed them. Arriving at her house, she didn't have to ask who had repaired her picture window. She knew.

Gingerly, she slid out of the vehicle, but before she took another step, he scooped her into his arms. "I'm capable of walking on my own two feet," she protested, privately appreciating his chivalry.

"Humor me." He walked inside, then nudged the front door shut with his shoe.

"I can manage, now," she said, expecting him to set her on her feet. Instead, he strode to the couch.

"You're not listening," she said, enjoying the experience of being held in his strong arms.

He gently lowered her onto the sofa. "I know."

The pain pill she'd taken before leaving the E.R. started to work. She began to feel drowsy and her tongue tangled over her words. "I wanna tell you som'thin' 'portant."

"We'll talk about it later. For now, just rest."

Comforted by his presence, Jenna dozed off as instructed.

❧

She ran through the corridor, hearing a maniacal laugh echo behind her. She had to find Jason. Where was he? She turned the corner and ran into a man—the very man she'd been trying to escape. "Jason!" she screamed.

"Jenna, wake up. It's only a bad dream."

The words repeated by a familiar voice finally penetrated the terror she'd relived. She released her bruising grip of his biceps. "I'm sorry. I guess I don't know my own strength."

"Don't be silly. Nightmares are common after an ordeal like yours." He held her for several minutes.

Jenna tucked her head under his chin. "What will happen to Harry?"

"He's headed for a psych unit and a mental evaluation. He'll either stay there for treatment or go to prison. Maybe both."

"Poor Lydia."

"Poor Bruce. He feels badly because he didn't make the connection between Harry and your phone caller. So do I, for that matter."

"You figured it out. That's what counts."

Jason squeezed her tightly. "I was so afraid I'd lose you. When I thought you were lying somewhere, hurt. . ." his voice faded. "I love you too much to let you walk away from me for any reason. Those hours you were missing emphasized how empty I'd be without you, regardless of how many others join our family."

She raised her head to meet his gaze. Happy tears filled her eyes. "My life wouldn't be the same if you weren't a part of it."

"Love does cast out fear," he said. "Whatever God has in store for us, we can handle together."

"Are you sure, Jason?"

He nodded, looking thoughtful. "I can't arrange my life down to the last detail if I want God to lead me. I'm not saying we can't make plans, but I think we have to be flexible enough and sensitive enough to the Lord's leading so we can do His will. Otherwise, we're doing what we want instead of letting the Lord be in control."

Jenna hugged him. "You're right. Now I understand why I've always been drawn to Proverbs 3:5, 'Trust in the Lord with all your heart, and lean not unto thine own understanding.' With Him guiding us, we can't go wrong."

His expression became hopeful. "With those details worked out, will you marry me?"

She smiled. "You've stolen my heart. I can't possibly refuse."

epilogue

Three years later

Jason dumped his briefcase on the kitchen table. The house was quiet and he wondered where Jenna might be. Listening carefully, he heard his wife's voice and a small, high-pitched laugh coming through the open window above the kitchen sink.

Staring into the back yard, he reveled in the sight of Jenna pushing their eighteen-month-old son, Ryan, in the baby swing. The toddler shrieked with delight as the contraption sailed through the air.

His brother, Lance, had been responsible for adding Ryan to the Daly family. While Jenna pursued a medical solution, Jason had sworn Lance to secrecy and asked him to arrange a private adoption.

He smiled, remembering her expression when he handed her a large manila envelope on an otherwise unremarkable day. She'd read the papers through twice before she dropped them on the floor and hugged the stuffing out of him.

He didn't regret his decision to adopt at all; he was too busy thanking God for his son and for His faithfulness. Feeling secure with Lance handling the details, he was ready to take another chance.

Jason stepped onto the patio.

"Dadda!" a tiny voice screeched.

"Hiya bud. How've you been today?"

Jenna stopped the swing, handed Ryan to his father, then kissed her husband. "Is it five o'clock already?"

"No, I'm home early. Ryan, what did you and Mommy do all day?"

Ryan answered in gurgles and grunts, waving his chubby arms.

Jason recognized one word. "You and Mommy went shopping?"

Ryan tugged on his father's nose and chortled.

Jenna followed them into the living room. "It's hot today. Want something cold to drink?"

"In a minute." He sat on the sofa and bounced Ryan on one knee. "First, I have something to tell you."

"Oh?"

"Susan Hill is coming. She'll be here any time."

She sank onto the cushion beside him. "Why?"

"Remember when we filled out those papers months ago in order to adopt an older child?" At her nod, he continued. "She called yesterday and asked if we'd be interested in taking two children, a boy who's five and his three-year-old sister. I said—"

"Jason, you can't mean it. Two more?"

The first twinge of doubt struck him. Perhaps he hadn't made such a wise decision. "Honey, Susan doesn't want to split them up. If you don't want—"

"No." She jumped to her feet. "It's wonderful. Ryan will have a brother and a sister."

The doorbell rang. Jenna's face registered her excitement as he passed Ryan to her before greeting their visitors.

Susan waited on the porch, holding the left hand of a dark-headed boy and the right hand of a smaller, feminine version. "Jenna and Jason? I'd like you to meet David and Ashley."

Not to be left out, Ryan screamed his welcome while a toothy smile spread across his face.

"Baby?" Ashley broke loose to approach Ryan and stare up at him.

Jenna crouched down to her eye level. "His name is Ryan." Ashley gently touched his dark brown curls while Ryan grabbed at her shiny barrette. David came closer. Before long, all three were playing on the floor.

By the time Susan left, both children had agreed to stay with the Dalys.

Jason carried the youngsters' meager belongings to a spare bedroom. He returned to find his wife staring at the little group. Glistening tears threatened to spill from her eyes.

"I never dreamed—" she cut herself off. "How did you arrange this? And today of all days."

He slid his arms around her waist and hugged her. "I put in a special request and the Lord answered my prayer. Happy anniversary, darling."

A Letter To Our Readers

Dear Reader:

In order that we might better contribute to your reading enjoyment, we would appreciate your taking a few minutes to respond to the following questions. When completed, please return to the following:

Rebecca Germany, Managing Editor
Heartsong Presents
P.O. Box 719
Uhrichsville, Ohio 44683

1. Did you enjoy reading *Thief of My Heart?*
   ❑ Very much. I would like to see more books
      by this author!
   ❑ Moderately
      I would have enjoyed it more if _____

   _____

2. Are you a member of **Heartsong Presents**? ❑Yes ❑No
   If no, where did you purchase this book? _____

   _____

3. What influenced your decision to purchase this
   book? (Check those that apply.)

   ❑ Cover   ❑ Back cover copy

   ❑ Title   ❑ Friends

   ❑ Publicity   ❑ Other_____

4. How would you rate, on a scale from 1 (poor) to 5
   (superior), the cover design? _____

5. On a scale from 1 (poor) to 10 (superior), please rate the following elements.

    __Heroine   __Plot

    __Hero   __Inspirational theme

    __Setting   __Secondary characters

6. What settings would you like to see covered in **Heartsong Presents** books?_____

_____

_____

7. What are some inspirational themes you would like to see treated in future books?_____

_____

_____

8. Would you be interested in reading other **Heartsong Presents** titles?   ❏ Yes   ❏ No

9. Please check your age range:
  ❏ Under 18   ❏ 18-24   ❏ 25-34
  ❏ 35-45   ❏ 46-55   ❏ Over 55

10. How many hours per week do you read? _____

Name _____

Occupation _____

Address _____

City _____ State _____ Zip _____

Summer Dreams

*Four all-new inspirational novellas
with all the romance of a summer's day.*

Summer Breezes by **Veda Boyd Jones**
Law school graduate Melina Howard takes on Blake Allen, a
former sailing instructor, as her crew in a local regatta.

A la Mode by **Yvonne Lehman**
Small town florist Heather Willis is intrigued when she makes
the acquaintance of a mysterious stranger with a Texan accent.

King of Hearts by **Tracie J. Peterson**
Elise Jost is a non-traditional student whose life's direction
takes a different course when she makes a high grade with
professor Ian Hunter.

No Groom for the Wedding by **Kathleen Yapp**
A professional photographer, Penny Blake is capturing her
sister's honeymoon when she finds herself the focus of a fellow
cruise passenger.

(352 pages, Paperbound, 5" x 8")

···· Presents ····

Great Inspirational Romance at a Great Price!

Heartsong Presents books are inspirational romances in contemporary and historical settings, designed to give you an enjoyable, spirit-lifting reading experience. You can choose wonderfully written titles from some of today's best authors like Veda Boyd Jones, Yvonne Lehman, Tracie J. Peterson, Nancy N. Rue, and many others.

When ordering quantities less than twelve, above titles are $2.95 each.